Lawman For Slaughter Valley

Lawman For Slaughter Valley

RAY HOGAN

Sagebrush
Large Print Westerns

Library of Congress Cataloging-in-Publication Data

Hogan, Ray, 1908-
    Lawman for Slaughter Valley / Ray Hogan.
      p. cm.
    ISBN 1-57490-547-3 (alk. paper)
  1. Large type books. I. Title.

PS3558.O3473L298 2004
 813'.54—dc22   2003028319

The Cataloging in Publication Data was not available at time of publication.

Cataloging in Publication Data is available from
the British Library and the National Library of Australia.

Sagebrush Large Print Westerns are published in the United States and Canada by Thomas T. Beeler, Publisher, PO Box 310, Rollinsford, New Hampshire 03869-0310. ISBN 1-57490-547-3 Published in the United Kingdom, Eire, and the Republic of South Africa by Isis Publishing Ltd, 7 Centremead, Osney Mead, Oxford OX2 0ES England. ISBN 0-7531-7106-6

Published in Australia and New Zealand by Bolinda Publishing Pty Ltd, 17 Mohr Street, Tullamarine, Victoria, Australia, 3043 ISBN 1-7409-3262-5

Manufactured by Sheridan Books in Chelsea, Michigan.

1

STARBUCK DREW HIS HORSE TO A HALT in the warm afternoon sunlight and studied the faded sign facing him from the edge of the road . . . TANNEKAW. He sighed, wiping at the film of gray dust on his weather-burned features. Another town. Would his luck be any better there than it had been in all the other places he had visited in his search for Ben?

He had entertained high hopes that he would find his brother in Santa Fe, had actually changed his original plan of spending only a few days in the ancient capital and had extended his stay through the winter, in the belief that Ben, attracted by the colorful festivities that marked the Christmas season in the old city, would put in an appearance.

The possibility proved groundless, and shortly after the holidays ended Starbuck rode on, following the time-worn trail that, if pursued, would lead a man all the way to Mexico City.

On the first day out he paused briefly in the settlement of Bernalillo, on the banks of the Rio Grande, near where Spanish conquerors had spent a bloody winter some three centuries earlier, ruthlessly teaching their red-skinned subjects the advantages of royalist civilization.

Having no luck there, he continued south, soon arriving at another small town situated on the same river and hemmed in by towering mountains on the east and a wall of extinct volcanoes on the west. It was again an unproductive pause. No one there had ever heard of Ben Starbuck, or of Damon Friend, a name Shawn thought his brother might be using; nor could anyone recall having noticed a pilgrim who fitted the meager description he was able to give of his brother.

In the saddle again, he followed the winding stream as it made its way on down the floor of the valley, stirring now under the promise of spring, past a sunbaked pueblo of friendly Indians and a half a dozen more small villages, until he reached, finally, the town of Socorro at the upper end of that dreaded hell on earth, the awesome *Jornado del Muerto*.

He found some encouragement in Socorro. Although the lawman had no recollection of his brother under any name, he suggested Shawn try the Slaughter Valley country, on to the southwest. It was an area of big ranches rimming the town of Tannekaw, and a great deal of hiring of new hands was being done. If Ben worked cattle and was looking for a job, the chances were better than good that he'd sign on with one of the Slaughter Valley outfits.

Starbuck had taken the sheriff's suggestion, heading out the next day, pointing first for the Seven Brothers Mountains since that route was said to be faster as well as safer. From there he angled through a maze of rocks that went on for miles, and then crossed the greening plains of Burro Mountain until at last he was in the Slaughter Valley country. The name had puzzled him at first; he had known a man in Arizona Territory—a rancher whose name was Slaughter—and wondered if he had moved or extended his interests.

There was no connection, the Socorro lawman had assured him. The valley took its name from a massacre—one involving an incident between a band of Apache warriors and a California-bound wagon train.

He'd headquarter there, at Tannekaw, he decided,

2

looking ahead at the scatter of buildings lying silent in the bright sunshine. He'd get a line on all of the ranches and visit them one by one, making his inquiries concerning Ben. It could take a week, perhaps two, and if he met with the usual failure, he'd move on to Tucson.

It was a routine now grown old to Shawn Starbuck. He had wandered from town to town—from the Mexican border north to Canada, from the Mississippi west to the vast Pacific—sometimes coming close but always finding disappointment at the end of the trail he had followed.

Bitterness at such failure had long since given way to a quiet sort of resignation; one day he would find Ben, alive or perhaps dead—but he would find him and the quest would then end. That he could spend his lifetime searching—waste it, in fact, as some had prophesied— was possible, but he gave that only occasional thought. If that was to be his destiny, so be it; he would accept it, for he felt he had no alternative. Yet there were times when his spirit hungered, moments when loneliness closed in upon him, and gripping him in a viselike clamp, turned him inward.

He was a man with the faint mark of youth still upon him despite a remoteness that tempering experience had brought. He brushed again at his face, and shifted on his saddle. Reaching down, he slid the heavy forty-five strapped to his left leg forward to a more comfortable position and clucked softly to the big sorrel gelding. Might as well move on, get to the hotel and line up a room. He'd start asking questions there; perhaps the clerk would know something of Ben. Perhaps . . .

He moved on at a slow pace, crossed a small flat, and reached the end of the street. He swung into it, noting

3

again its deserted appearance. It seemed unusual, for summer's intense heat had not yet set in dictating the hours for shopping and conducting business, but he had long ago ceased to be surprised by the different customs encountered in different settlements. There would be a reason for the absence of activity, he knew.

To his left he noted a small white church set well back from the roadway. Its adjoining cemetery was clean of weeds and orderly, with all of the grassy mounds neatly tended and bearing markers. Gus Damson's livery barn was first in the line of structures on the west side of the street, and directly opposite, in rapid succession, lay the Blue Ribbon Bakery, Miss Purdy's Ladies' & Children's Clothing Store, a vacant building, Corrigan's Gun Shop, Henry Grissom's General Store, and the marshal's office.

Shawn mentally fixed the location of the lawman's quarters in his mind. He'd make a call on the marshal after he'd arranged for a room at the hotel. Raising his glance, he squinted into the glare, scanning the facades for a hostelry. He located it just beyond the lawman's office on the opposite side of the broad lane. It was a bulky, two-storied structure called the Far West. It had a full-width porch, and there was a stable behind it, he saw with satisfaction; he'd make use of it rather than Damson's. It would be much handier.

His idle inventory continued; Sol Wiseman, Gent's Clothing, a combination barber and undertaker, Bridger's Saddle & Harness Shop, the Lone Star Café, a residence or two, a small saloon called the Red Mule.

That completed the business establishments on the east wall of the canyon-like area separating the opposing structures. On the west side, which seemed to enjoy a lesser degree of preference, there were only

4

Damson's barn, the Lone Star, another small saloon, a couple of offices, several vacant storerooms, the hotel, and what appeared to be the largest building in town, the Valley Queen—Gambling, Dancing, and Liquors.

Farther on, and somewhat removed from the business district and the residences scattered on the outskirts, Shawn could see a two-floored frame house; the local bawdy establishment Shawn assumed, judging from its outward appearance.

He could see people inside the stores, many of them pausing to stare curiously at him as he rode by, heading for the hitchrack fronting the Far West, and he caught sight of a few persons working in their small, backyard gardens, but the town itself seemed to have drawn within.

He felt the hostility in the air before he was halfway to his intended destination. Tannekaw was awaiting something—trouble, likely, and that thought brought a frown to his features and stirred into life within him a current of impatience.

He'd like—just this once—to stay clear of other people's problems. Such involvement was forever occurring, delaying him in the pursuit of his own purpose, and while his upbringing at the hands of Hiram and Clare Starbuck had instilled in him a sense of responsibility toward the trouble-beset, he would have liked, this one time, to go about his business without interruption and complication.

It would take days to pay calls on all of the ranchers in Slaughter Valley, assuming he learned nothing of value from the merchants in Tannekaw, and should there be no trace of Ben at any of the ranches, he should move on to Tucson, where considerable work was in progress, as soon as possible.

Starbuck grinned wryly. He'd made such vows to himself before, declarations that he'd not permit himself to become involved; he had yet to keep those vows. Somehow he always found it impossible to turn his back on a man who asked him for help. He supposed that since the time he had first ridden out from the cold Starbuck home along Ohio's Muskingum River, he had given up in total a good half year to others, if all the days were added together into a single lump.

And during those days the search for Ben had gone begging. There could have even been times when his brother was near, perhaps in the next town, and arriving a week or two late may have caused him to miss out. It was something he never knew for certain, but quite often it caused him to wonder.

It would not happen in Tannekaw. He would attend strictly to his own business; he'd find out as quickly as is possible if Ben was in the Slaughter Valley country, and if he was not, he'd light out for Tucson, get there while things were still humming. For once he'd not arrive at a destination days later than planned.

He drew up to the rack of the Far West and again let his glance sweep the empty street. After a moment he swung off the saddle, grunting a little as his heels hit solid ground and the muscles of his back and legs made known their grateful relief at the change. It had been a long day, one that had started well before sunrise, and he had pushed the sorrel continually in an effort to reach the settlement before dark. A good meal and a soft bed both would be more than welcome.

Tugging at the strings behind the cantle, Shawn freed his blanket roll and saddlebags, hung them over his shoulder, and then winding the gelding's reins around the crossbar, started up the steps of the porch of the

6

hotel. He'd see to a room first, be sure one was available; then he'd return and arrange for the big gelding's care.

He paused. A dozen riders had turned into the lower end of the street. All were purposeful, hard-set men. Starbuck considered them thoughtfully. He reckoned he was looking at the reason why Tannekaw had sought shelter, had drawn inward.

2

STARBUCK, LOOMING TALL AND WIDE-SHOULDERED in the shadow of the saloon, lowered his gear to the top step and turned to watch. Except for the pair in the lead, the riders appeared to be ordinary working cowhands, leaning, perhaps, a bit to the tough, wild side. They curved in toward the jail, halted, then formed a half-circle facing it. The two in the front came off their horses lazily, indifferently.

The husky one, a thick necked, dark-faced man with small eyes, wearing a dirty undershirt beneath a stained leather vest, denim pants, and scarred work boots, brushed his hat to the back of his head and nodded to the men behind him.

"Don't figure this'll take long, boys. You all stay mounted . . . Me and Letterman'll handle it."

The puncher in the center of the semi-circle raised his hand in a gesture of understanding. "Yes, sir, Mr. Eagle," he said, and eased back in his saddle.

Letterman was evidently a hired gun, Shawn thought, studying the man idly. He was lean, quiet-faced, stood by silently, legs spread, as Eagle, probably one of the big ranchers in Slaughter Valley, called the shots.

"Bishop!" he yelled suddenly, swinging his attention to the marshal's office. "Come on out where I can do some talking to you!"

There was no response. Farther down the empty street a dog began to bark. Eagle took a few steps closer to the building, and Letterman also moved forward while still maintaining a position one pace behind the squat man.

"Bishop! Goddammit, I know you're in there! You

better get out here!"

There was motion just within the doorway of the low-roofed structure. A man wearing a star stepped slowly into view, halting on the landing outside. He was young to be a lawman, had thick brown hair that lay loose about his head, and eyes that darted nervously over the men ranged before him. His manner was anxious, almost one of desperation.

Eagle surveyed him with disdain for several moments, then shrugged. "Come after Jimmy Joe and Kansas," he drawled. "Hell—you known better'n to lock up any of my boys."

The marshal shifted uncertainly, dropping his glance. After a bit he shook his head. "They're paying a fine or serving time," he said in a low voice.

"Reckon not. What're they in for?"

"Disturbing the peace. Breaking up property."

"You talking about that little funning they was having in the Red Mule?"

"Was a fight. They done quite a lot of damage—and they were shooting off their guns. Could've hurt somebody."

"But they didn't, and far as damage is concerned, that outfit's made plenty off Longhorn cowhands—more'n enough to pay for what damage they done."

"Makes no difference. The law says—"

"The hell with the law!" Eagle snapped. "I'm all the law my boys need. Now, are you turning them loose or am I going in there after them? Brought me along enough help to take that crackerbox apart board by board if I have to."

Bishop slid a glance up the hushed street. His features were taut and his eyes were bright, reflecting the strain he was under.

9

"They got to serve out their terms, unless you're willing to pay the fines," he said stubbornly.

"Ain't about to!" Eagle snarled, yanking at his hat. "Who said they had to do all that? There ain't been no judge around here for months."

"It's a town ordinance-law. Disturbing the peace is ten days in jail, or a ten-dollar fine."

The squat rancher laughed, and threw a glance over his shoulder to the men behind him. "Well, I got a ordinance of my own. Says that nobody working for me ever lays out in jail or pays a fine—not in this town . . . All right, boys, let's go—"

"Hold on a minute!"

Eagle paused. Starbuck shifted his attention to the porch of the general store. A graying, middle-aged man wearing a bib apron over his work clothes crossed hurriedly to the steps and moved down into the street. The cowhands eased back in their saddles as Eagle raised a staying hand and grinned at the merchant.

"Well now, Mister Mayor, you got something you're wanting to say?"

This would be Henry Grissom, the store owner, Shawn supposed. Evidently he was also the mayor of the settlement.

"Like to talk a bit to the marshal," he said, walking rapidly toward the jail. "No reason why this can't all be ironed out with no trouble."

"No reason at all," Eagle said mildly. "All Bishop's got to do is turn my boys loose."

Grissom bobbed agreeably, and stepping up onto the landing, grasped the lawman by the arm and pushed him back into the building.

One of the punchers laughed. Letterman, a silent shadow throughout the exchange, nodded to Eagle.

10

"Seems the mayor don't want his jail tore up. Expect he'll straighten out the marshal."

"Just what he sure better do," the rancher replied, grinning.

The barking dog, emboldened by no show of opposition on the part of the riders, had slunk in closer. He was now in the center of the street, where he continued his frantic yapping. Eagle drew his pistol, snapping a shot at the animal. The bullet struck short, spurted dust over the mongrel. He yelped, turned tail, and raced off into the passageway that lay between the saddle shop and the Lone Star Café.

Grissom appeared at once in the doorway of the marshal's office. "They're coming right out, Mr. Eagle!" he shouted in an anxious tone as he glanced worriedly, up and down the street. "Won't be but a couple of seconds!"

The squat rancher holstered his weapon. He shook his head at Letterman. "Expect I'd best be sharpening up my aim, eh, Jack?"

Letterman shrugged. "Don't figure you was wanting to hit him. I've seen you do better'n that."

"Guess not," Eagle replied. "Always did sort of like dogs."

He turned to the jail as two punchers shuffled sheepishly out onto the landing, buckling on their gun belts as they came.

Grissom, following close behind like a mother hen seeing to her chicks, laid a hand on a shoulder of each. "Your horses were took to Gus Damson's stable. They've been looked after—he won't charge you nothing!" the merchant added hastily as the taller of the pair half came about, frowning. "Town'll pay for it."

"Reckon that's it, boys," Eagle cut in, facing the

11

riders still mounted. "You take these here little lost lambs and get them back to the ranch. There's plenty of work to be done. Me and Jack'll be along a bit later."

One of the freed prisoners paused, nodded to the rancher. "We sure are much obliged to you, Mr. Eagle—"

"You ought to be, me bailing you out of that there jail and away from that marshal. They plain don't come no tougher'n him!"

The puncher stared, and then as Eagle's dark face broke into a broad smile, he laughed, slapping his partner on the back.

"Yes, sir, that's the plain truth," he said, and swinging up behind one of the riders, moved off with the rest of the party for Damson's.

Starbuck watched the rancher glance toward Grissom. "Figured you'd be smart," he said.

The merchant nodded almost imperceptibly. "You got to understand—"

"Ain't nothing I got to do!" Eagle snapped, gathering up the reins of his horse. "Let's go, Jack."

Pivoting, and with Letterman close by, he headed back across the street for the Valley Queen saloon, standing just beyond the hotel. There was no mistaking the meaning in the rancher's words or the look he had given Henry Grissom; the mayor had been given definite warning that such an incident was not to occur again.

The merchant continued to study the two men in silence as they drew up to the Valley Queen's hitchrack, tethered their mounts, and stepped up onto the porch. They paused at the swinging doors briefly to scan the street, still deserted except for Grissom's slump-shouldered figure, and then disappeared inside.

Immediately, the merchant wheeled about and reentered the marshal's office, hurrying, undoubtedly to relay the rancher's warning to Bishop.

Shrugging, Starbuck picked up his gear and moved on toward the hotel's entrance. The law in Tannekaw had problems, it would seem.

3

HE REACHED THE SCREEN DOOR, hesitated as it swung open. Nodding, Shawn stepped in, glancing at the man who was admitting him. Elderly, freckle-faced, and red-haired, his features were set. Apparently he had been standing there viewing the confrontation in the street, and found it not to his liking.

"Afternoon," he murmured as Starbuck moved by him.

Shawn returned the greeting and continued on across the small lobby, with its heavy chairs and dusty table strewn with yellowing magazines, to the counter stationed in a back corner. To his right, through an arched opening draped with thick, green portieres, he could see a dining room. There were no patrons.

"Needing a room?" the red-haired man asked, slipping in behind the desk.

Starbuck nodded, propping his gear against a nearby chair. Accepting a stub of pencil, he bent over the well-thumbed book that had been pushed at him and wrote his name. He thought for a moment, and then in the column requiring his home address, put down Santa Fe. It would serve as well as any—and he had remained there longer than he ordinarily did in the towns he visited.

The clerk reversed the register, and read aloud: "Shawn Starbuck," and offered his hand. "Pleased to know you. I'm Clint Albers—own this place. Want you to know you're welcome here."

He half turned, and plucked a key from several hanging on a board nailed to the wall. "I'm giving you

14

Number Five. Nice, quiet room. Figure to stay long?"

Shawn said, "Few days. Maybe a week. Not sure."

Albers frowned, gestured toward the street. "Don't let that little misunderstanding scare you off. Likely won't ever happen again."

"It's not bothering me any. I'm here on a matter of personal business. But now that you mention it, I'd say the marshal got the hot end of the poker."

"Expect it does look that way."

"Who's the one they called Eagle?"

"Rancher. Got a place west of here. Longhorn's not the biggest in the valley, maybe, but I reckon everybody'll say it's the toughest."

"I got that idea from watching," Starbuck said dryly.

Albers ran long fingers through his thinning hair. "It was a mistake for Bishop—the marshal—to jug them two Longhorn cowboys," he said, shaking his head. "Should have known it would cause trouble."

"Heard him say they broke the law. Looking after it is his job."

"Ain't denying that, but a man's got to use a mite of common sense."

"Meaning this Eagle—"

"Ward Eagle's his full name."

"Meaning he's to be treated special—him and his aired hands?"

Clint Albers shrugged. "Well, maybe it does look that way to you, but it's usually best to make allowances when you're dealing with a bunch like those from Longhorn."

"They the only ones getting special treatment?"

"No, not exactly. Boys from other ranches come in, sort of have themselves a big time, too, only they maybe ain't as wild as Ward Eagle's crew."

15

"They'll get wilder now. What happened out there was the same as opening the gate."

"No doubt," the hotel man said morosely. "And it'll all come because of that fool Bishop. Other marshals we've had got along all right with them. Just let them have their fun, and everybody was satisfied. Bishop's new on the job—and he's young. Told Grissom, he's the mayor, the man you saw coming over to talk to the marshal—that he'd had experience. I'm doubting that."

"Maybe having the ground cut out from under him is what's new."

Albers frowned, tugging at a tip of his reddish mustache. "Could be. You some kind of a lawman?"

Starbuck said, "No, not now. Have done a few turns wearing a star."

"Well, what Grissom did was for the good of their town. Long as we can keep that wild bunch doing their hell-raising in the saloons we'll be all right. Expect was a favor to Arlie Bishop, too. Like as not he'd've got himself killed bucking Eagle and Jack Letterman in the way he was starting to do."

"Is Letterman a hired gun?"

"Supposed to be the foreman of Longhorn, but you always see him siding Ward, standing around like he was just waiting to use his gun. Any chance you'd be interested in taking on the marshal's job? Won't surprise me none to see him pull out. Expect, was I to talk to Grissom, he'd be more'n happy—"

"Obliged to you," Shawn cut in before Albers could complete the proposal, "but, like I mentioned, I'm here on personal business."

"Something to do with the town?"

"No, I'm looking for my brother."

The hotel owner frowned, pursing his lips. "Starbuck?

16

Don't recollect ever hearing the name before.

"Yeh, Ben Starbuck. Could be calling himself Damon Friend."

Albers was again thoughtful. Finally, he shook his head. "Don't ring no bells—neither name. What's he look like?"

"Probably a bit shorter than me, and maybe heavier. Hair ought to be dark and his eyes a sharp blue, but that could've changed."

"Sounds like you don't know much about him yourself."

"That's about right. It's been quite a spell since I last saw him—when we were kids. Main thing I've go to go on is a scar."

"I see. What makes you think he's here in Tannekaw?"

"Not sure he is. I'm only looking and hoping. I heard there was quite a bit of cow work going on in the valley, and figured he might've hired on at one of the ranches."

"Good chance of that," Albers said. "And a good chance, too, I'd never run across him, being in the hotel business. Cowhands don't rent rooms when they come to town. Spend their time and money in one of the saloons—or maybe at Ruby McGrath's place."

"That the big house on the corner, standing back from the street?"

"That's it. If you're hunting female company that's the place to go. I was noticing that belt buckle you're wearing. It mean you're a champion fighter—one of them boxer kind?"

Shawn glanced down at the oblong of scrolled silver with the ivory figure of a boxer in customary pose set in its center. "Belonged to my pa. I started wearing it after he died."

17

"You know how to fight that way?"

"He taught both Ben and me. I saw you had a stable out back. Like to put my horse there."

"Sure enough, I'll see he's taken care of. Got a right good restaurant, too—here in the building. Woman cook."

"I'll give it a try," Starbuck said, picking up his gear.

"Sorry I couldn't help you none with your brother, but like I said, not much chance of him coming in here. Place for you to ask questions is in the saloons. I'd try Rufe Hagerty first. Runs the Valley Queen—next door. If he can't help you, then go over to the Red Mule and the Silver Dollar—back up the street, near Gus Damson's livery barn."

"Noticed it when I rode in," Shawn said, pausing.

He turned, and stared across the lobby, through the dust-clogged screen door, into the street. It was still early. He might as well walk over to the Valley Queen before he went to his room. Not only could he talk with Rufe Hagerty, but with Ward Eagle as well. After all, he was one of the Slaughter Valley ranchers and it was possible Ben could be working for him.

"Think I'll do that right now," he said, again depositing his gear against the chair.

"Sure, you go right ahead," Albers said. "I'll stash your duffle for you and tell the hostler to look after your horse. Don't forget about my restaurant when you're ready to eat."

Starbuck nodded and turned for the door.

18

4

HENRY GRISSOM WAS JUST EMERGING from the marshal's office as Shawn stepped out onto the hotel's veranda. Head down, the merchant returned slowly to his place of business. Starbuck could see Bishop, inside the jail, slumped in a chair behind a desk. Being the marshal in a town where law was bent to accommodate certain privileged persons had to be a frustrating task.

Moving down to street level, Shawn covered the short distance to the front of the Valley Queen. As he mounted the steps he swept the opposing rows of buildings with a calculating glance. Mayor Grissom, his civic duty executed, was now attending to business. A few persons, the emergency over, were now to be seen on the sidewalks. Evidently all had expected the meeting between Ward Eagle and Marshal Bishop to be much more violent that it had proven to be. He guessed that was because the lawman was new on the job, and Tannekaw residents were not certain of his abilities.

Elbowing his way through the swinging doors, Shawn entered the dimly lit saloon and walked slowly toward the bar—a long counter placed against the wall opposite the entrance. Eagle and Letterman were the only customers at it, but there were three riders in a back corner who were engaged in a desultory game of cards around one of the tables.

The man behind the counter, a balding, paunchy individual with piercing blue eyes, greeted him with nod and said, "What'll it be?"

"Rye," Starbuck replied, and shifted his attention to Eagle and Jack Letterman, who had paused to consider him speculatively. He returned their gaze with a steady coolness, and after a moment both turned back and resumed their conversation.

"Rye it is," the bartender said, placing a brimming shot glass in front of Shawn. "Just passing through?"

"That's about the way of it. You Rufe Hagerty?"

The balding man's brows lifted. "So I'm told. Something I can do for you?"

"Looking for my brother. Albers—over at the hotel said maybe you could help."

"Lot of folks come in here. Some I know, some are strangers. What's he called?"

"Ben Starbuck, or maybe Damon Friend," Shawn said, and gave his description.

"Which one's the real name?"

"Starbuck. Figured he might be working on one of the ranches around here."

Hagerty polished the counter before him with a damp cloth. Like most saloon owners, he tended bar himself during the day when business was light, had hired help to take over at night when the crowd was large and his attention was needed elsewhere.

"Possible," he said. "Can't say as I recall either one of the names or anybody jibing with the description you give. Lot of strangers around, however."

"Rufe, how about another bottle?" Eagle cut in loudly. "Or maybe you're too busy yammering with that drifter to wait on your regular customers."

Hagerty's jaw tightened. He gave Shawn an apologetic look, as if asking him to ignore the rancher's words, and moved away. Reaching under the bar he produced a full quart of whiskey and set it before the two men.

"Who's your friend?" Eagle asked, wrapping his

20

thick fingers around the neck of the bottle. He made no effort to lower his voice.

"Name's Starbuck," Hagerty answered. "Come here looking for his brother. Figures he might be working for one of the outfits in the valley."

"Not for me," the rancher said, pulling the cork from the bottle with his teeth and filling the glasses before him. "Got the same crew I had last year. Man hires on with me, he stays hired on."

"His choice or yours?" Starbuck asked coolly, his anger aroused by Eagle's overbearing attitude.

The rancher hesitated, frowning. He'd had too much to drink and was taking on more. "What's that mean?" he demanded.

"Just a question," Starbuck said. "Forget it."

Ward Eagle set the bottle back on the counter, bobbed his head in satisfaction, and faced the wordless Letterman.

"Mighty lucky for that jasper that he pulled in his horns. Ain't in no mood to take any sass—not from nobody."

Eagle's foreman nodded, and as the rancher tipped back his head to drink, he surreptitiously emptied his glass in the cuspidor near his booted foot.

Hagerty, worry clouding his eyes, returned to Shawn. "Obliged to you for overlooking what he said."

Starbuck shrugged. "He's drunk."

"And getting worse. You see what happened out there in the street? That row with the marshal, I mean."

Shawn said, "I was watching from the hotel."

"Afraid it ain't over yet. Eagle—that's who that is— is getting uglier by the minute."

"Cut off his whiskey."

The saloonman's brows lifted again. He smiled

21

ruefully. "You don't cut off Ward Eagle's whiskey," he said.

"Seems to be a big man around here."

"Don't you ever doubt it," Hagerty said, keeping his voice low. "Throws his weight around plenty—and makes folks like it. Ain't only that he's a hardcase; about half the crew working for him are toughs— onetime outlaws and—"

"What'd you say your name was?" the rancher broke in loudly, wheeling to face Shawn.

"Starbuck—"

"Starbuck—that's a hell of a name. You looking for a job?"

"No, for my brother."

"Oh, yeh, Hagerty was telling me. You see me buffalo that two-bit lawman out there a while ago?"

Shawn nodded.

Eagle hooked his elbows on the edge of the bar and spat. "Good thing for him he didn't try nothing. I'd a cut him down for sure."

"Be no chore, not with all the help you brought along," Starbuck said dryly.

The rancher bristled. "Help? You meaning Jack here and them boys that rode in with me? Hell, they come to do some watching. I don't need them. Don't need nobody. Always done my own snake skinning."

Shawn pushed his glass toward Rufe Hagerty for a refill. Eagle's head came forward belligerently.

"You savvy?"

The hush that filled the saloon was complete. Starbuck answered, "I heard what you said."

"You a friend of that badge-toter?"

Shawn took up his glass and studied its contents. "No, never saw him—or you—before today."

22

"Then why the hell are you taking up for him?"

Jack Letterman laid a hand on the rancher's shoulder and gently brought him back around. "He ain't taking up for him, Ward," he said softly. "What say we mount up and head for the ranch?"

Eagle shook off his foreman. "I ain't ready yet—same as I ain't done with that marshal. Aim to teach him a lesson he won't forget. He's going to know that none of my boys is ever to be throwed in that jail again."

"Reckon he understands that," Letterman said. "No use riding him into the ground."

"The hell there ain't! Want him and the rest of this here town to remember just who the he-bull in this country is! Reason I'm big as I am. Don't believe in letting folks forget."

"No need to—"

"Just you mind your drinking and leave everything else to me," the rancher snapped. "By the time I ride out of here today, there won't be nobody in the whole damned valley who'll ever take the notion to buck me again."

Shawn sipped at his whiskey. Ward Eagle had forgotten him during the heat of the moment, and the danger of a quarrel was past. He raised his eyes to Rufe Hagerty. The saloon owner wagged his head.

"Sure wish Jack could talk him into going home," he murmured.

"Now's when you could use a good lawman—one that's not afraid of having the rug pulled out from under him."

"For a fact," Hagerty said. "Now, about this brother of yours; where else have you asked?"

"Only at the hotel."

"Then best thing you can do is walk over to the Red

23

Mule. If you don't have no luck there, try Ruby McGrath's place—it's just across the street. Then there's the Silver Dollar, up at the other end of town. If he's around here, somebody in one of them will know him—that is unless he don't do no drinking or womaning."

Shawn smiled faintly. "Haven't seen him in a long time but I doubt if he's turned into a saint."

"If it happens you don't have no luck, drop back by here and I'll give you the names of the—"

"Want you all to come, do some watching," Eagle said, raising his voice to include not only Starbuck and Hagerty but the card players in the far corner of the room as well. "Want you to see me learn that marshal a little lesson."

Hagerty cast a quick, appealing glance at the Longhorn foreman. Letterman shrugged, admitting his helplessness.

"I figure if I was to put a notch in his ear, he'd have hisself a reminder to leave all Longhorn boys alone and mind his own p's and q's."

"Why don't you let it pass, Ward?" Hagerty said. "You've made your point with him. Pushing it more ain't going to help none."

"It's going to help me!" the rancher shouted, shoving himself away from the counter and starting across the floor. "I'm plain itching to—" He paused, looking to the rear of the saloon through narrowing eyes. The men at the table had not stirred. Jerking out his pistol he fired a shot into the ceiling.

"You all hear me?" he demanded through the rocking echoes and drifting smoke. "Want you outside watching me!"

The card players kicked back their chairs and came

upright instantly. In single file they circled the table and moved toward the center of the saloon.

Ward Eagle bobbed his head approvingly. "That's better," he said and swung to Hagerty. "Means you, too, Rufe—and you, Starback—or whatever you call yourself. Being new around these parts, it'll be a good time for you to learn just who I am."

Shawn tipped his glass to his lips and drained it slowly as the rancher, followed closely by Jack Letterman, again swung to the doorway, his step much steadier than would be expected considering the amount of liquor he had consumed. Hagerty, holding off until the last, wheeled to fall in behind the card players.

"I'd like another shot of rye," Starbuck said indifferently, taking perverse satisfaction in being contrary.

The saloonman paused, turned back, and taking up the bottle, filled Shawn's glass. Eagle halted at the interruption and looked over his thick shoulder angrily.

"Goddammit you can do your drinking when I'm done!"

Letterman touched Starbuck with his cold eyes, then pushed gently at the rancher. "He's coming."

Finishing his drink, Shawn reached into his pocket. "How much?"

"Six bits'll do it," Hagerty replied hurriedly, and pocketing the coins Starbuck dropped onto the counter, took his place with the card players.

Shawn watched them cross to the batwings, and then shrugging, followed them out onto the porch.

5

WARD EAGLE, A STRIDE AHEAD OF LETTERMAN, stepped down into the dust of the street. Hitching at his gunbelt, he swaggered toward the lawman's office. Hagerty, halting just outside the swinging doors, muttered something, while the card players, walking softly, crossed to the end of the porch and quickly disappeared into the passageway between the saloon and the adjacent Far West Hotel.

Along the way a scattering of men had paused on the sidewalks to watch. Henry Grissom, venturing out onto the broad landing fronting his establishment, was considering Eagle with frowning intentness. If he suspected the rancher's purpose, he was making no effort to interfere.

"Marshal!"

At Eagle's loud summons a deeper quiet seemed to settle over the town. Rufe Hagerty turned a strained face to Shawn.

"This is going to be a hell of a thing," he said in a tight voice.

Starbuck nodded, moving forward until he was at the edge of the veranda. Within him a strong flow of caution was reminding him to stay clear of the impending trouble, to allow Marshal Bishop and the town to work out their problems with Eagle without his help.

"Marshal, you still in there?"

The sun's slanting rays struck against the squat figure of the rancher, casting a larger, dark shadow before him. Elsewhere along the way the glass store windows had

26

turned golden in the softening light.

"You better be coming out, Bishop, 'cause I'll come in after you if you don't! Aim to—"

The lawman was suddenly standing in the doorway. He held an old single-barreled shotgun in his hands and his face was chalk white. A worried frown corrugated his forehead, and as he brought his weapon up to waist level, the corners of his mouth twitched nervously.

Ward Eagle rocked back on his heels and laughed. "Figured that'd make you stir your stumps."

"What do you want?" Bishop said. His voice was high-pitched, unsteady.

"Why, I'm a-wanting you, Mister Tin Star. You got some learning to do."

"Leave me be," the lawman said wearily. "You got your men turned loose. Just go on your way."

"Just what I'm doing soon's I give you a little something to remember by."

"Remember what?"

"That you ain't to bother no Longhorn boys when they come to town, no matter what tomfoolishness they get into."

"I expect to do my job—"

"Your job's to leave them alone! I own this here town, and just so's you won't forget it, I'm going to put a notch in your ear!"

The heavy-gauge gun in the lawman's hands, already partially aimed, blasted the silence into a rolling wave of echoes. Ward Eagle, his pistol only half way out of its holster, was hurled backward, as if a mighty wind had slammed into him. Arms and legs flung wide, he sprawled in the dust. He had taken the full charge of buckshot in his chest.

For a fraction of time there was only the thundering

27

echoes, the hovering layers of smoke, and then Jack Letterman moved. His hand swept down for the pistol on his hip.

"Letterman—no!" Starbuck's voice crackled its warning as his own weapon came up fast. The man froze, fingers wrapped about the butt of his gun.

"One killing's enough," Shawn said coldly. "Forget it."

Longhorn's foreman straightened slowly, his hand falling away. Off to the left, Henry Grissom was running forward, while from farther away people were coming into view and moving hesitantly toward the limp, dusty shape of Ward Eagle lying crumpled in the sunlight.

Starbuck came down off the saloon's porch and crossed silently to where Letterman stood. Stepping in close, he lifted the foreman's weapon from its holster, methodically punched the cartridges from the cylinder, and kicked them into the loose dust. Returning the pistol to its leather sheath, he stepped back a pace.

"Get your horses and load him up," he ordered. "Then move on."

Jack Letterman, face dark, eyes glowing with anger, hesitated momentarily. Shawn cocked the hammer of his weapon, the clicks audible in the quiet. At once the man turned toward the hitchrack. Starbuck, eyeing him narrowly, backed to the front of the jail, where Bishop, slack and white-faced, sagged against the doorway.

"Get a hold of yourself," Starbuck said through tight lips. "That's a lawman's star you're wearing."

Bishop stirred, swallowed hard, drew himself up. The old shotgun, useless after its one load had been discharged, was still clutched in his right hand.

He propped it against the wall. A few steps away,

28

Henry Grissom looked on angrily.

Letterman, dark and sullen, led up the two horses, halting them beside the rancher's body. Ground-reining them, he turned and bent over Eagle. A man pushed forward from the steadily growing crowd to assist. Letterman shook his head, warning him back. Alone, he hoisted Eagle to his mount, draping him across the saddle, and then climbed onto his own horse. Seated, he gathered in the reins and turned to Bishop.

"This don't end here."

"It should," Starbuck said. "The man was a fool to draw with a cocked shotgun pointed at him." Letterman's expression did not change. "Makes no difference. He killed Ward. Max won't let that pass. Neither will the boys at the ranch."

Grissom abruptly found his voice. He pressed forward anxiously. "No need to tell him. Like the stranger says, Ward shouldn't've tried to draw."

A twisted grin pulled at the foreman's mouth. "Try explaining that to Max when he gets here," he said, and leading the rancher's horse, he swung about and headed off down the street.

The silence hung until he reached the corner beyond the Valley Queen and cut onto the road that led west, and then, as if on signal, a crescendo of voices rose. Grissom's features an angry red, his eyes snapping, he crossed to Bishop.

"You fool—you damned fool! What made you pull a stunt like that?"

Face still bleak, the lawman wagged his head helplessly. "I—I don't know. Was the only thing—"

"What did you expect him to do?" Starbuck asked, holstering his weapon and leaning back against the front of the jail. "Stand there and get his head blown off?"

"Ward wouldn't've killed him. He was only horsing around."

"That's plain foolishness," Shawn said, folding his arms. "He was drunk-enough to be dangerous. If he'd tried what he had in mind, he would've killed the marshal sure."

Grissom sighed deeply and looked off down the street. "Well, maybe so, but the fat's sure in the fire now. That Longhorn bunch'll tear this town apart, and when Max—"

"Heard Letterman mention him. Who is he?"

The merchant stared. "You mean you ain't never heard of Max Eagle?"

"Can't say that I have," Shawn answered, shaking his head.

"Then you sure are new to this part of the country. Figured everybody knew him. Gunfighter. Been told he's one of the fastest and best—and he's Ward's brother."

"Ain't nobody ever beat him yet!" a man in the crowd declared. "Plumb stupid to cross him. Fellow'd have a better chance playing patty-cake with a couple of rattlesnakes than he'd have going up against him."

"And that's what you're facing," Grissom said, pointing a long finger at Bishop.

A small sound escaped the lawman's throat. He wheeled suddenly, and stepping into his office, slammed the door.

Shawn stared at the weathered, wooden panel for a long moment and then turned to the crowd. "Show's over," he said, including Grissom in his words. "Go on about your business." Wheeling, he opened the door and entered the jail.

6

CLOSING THE DOOR BEHIND HIM, Starbuck halted, his glance on Marshal Arlie Bishop. The lawman was sitting in his chair, shoulders slumped, face lowered. At Shawn's entrance he looked up. Utter hopelessness filled his eyes.

In that same moment the latch behind Starbuck clicked, and he felt the impact of the door swinging into him. He stepped aside. Henry Grissom, taut with anger, burst into the room.

"Who the hell do you think you are?" he demanded, facing Shawn. "The way you go high-handing around here, a man'd think you owned the place!"

Starbuck reached out and closed the door once again. "I got the idea I'm the only friend the marshal has in this town," he said coolly.

Grissom's mouth drew into a down-curving line. "And who's fault is that? What he's done is enough to—"

"What he did was uphold the law—the thing you hired him to do and then didn't have the guts to back him up on."

"Ward Eagle's different. He knows that."

"There aren't supposed to be any exceptions. Law applies the same to every man—"

"Don't go spouting the law to me!" the merchant yelled. "I know what it says. Hell, I helped write it out when we started this town. But a man's got to use horse sense when it comes to enforcing it."

Starbuck shook his head. "You can't do it that way. If it applies to one man, it applies to the next."

Grissom swore deeply. "No point talking to you

31

about it—don't know why I am in the first place. You don't belong around here. Now, get out. There are a few things I've got to say to Bishop."

Starbuck shrugged and started to turn. Immediately, the lawman's head came up.

"I'm asking him to stay," he said dully.

The merchant's eyes snapped. "And I'm telling you to move on! Happens I'm running this town."

"I'm the marshal," Bishop said doggedly. "This is my jail and I got the say-so here."

"I can damn quick clear your ass out of here—fire you!"

"All you've got to do is tell me, and then you can pin this star on yourself."

Henry Grissom's lips parted to make a quick reply, but he paused, having second thoughts. He shook his head. "All right, it'll be your way. Reckon we do owe him a little, stopping lack Letterman the way he did. Thing could've got out of hand."

Shawn placed his shoulders against the door, crossing his arms. His firm resolution to keep out of another man's trouble had gone by the board, he realized, and he was getting sucked in deeper with each passing minute—but he'd had no choice. He couldn't just stand there and watch Letterman shoot down the marshal, helpless before him with an empty gun in his hands! An old, single-barreled scattergun—what kind of a fool was Bishop, anyway, grabbing up a weapon such as that with which to face a couple of hard cases like Eagle and Letterman?

Arlie Bishop *was* a fool, Shawn decided, eyeing the lawman. It was evident he had little if any experience, and that he was totally over his depth in the job. Why had he taken it? He must have realized he could never cope with the trigger-happy toughs with whom he was certain to come in contact; what then would prompt him to pass himself off as a lawman when he knew he could not stand up to the hazards of the profession?

"Want you understanding this, Bishop," Grissom was saying in a harsh voice. "The whole town's washing its hands of this mess. You stirred it up, now you face it."

Shawn supposed he could ride on—simply claim his gear at the hotel, saddle the sorrel, and pull out, get clear of the brewing trouble before it was too late. He had stepped in, kept Bishop alive through the crisis with Ward Eagle, now let someone else shoulder the chore.

After his example there surely was somebody around who thought enough of the law to back the marshal, despite Grissom. . . . But he wasn't ready to leave; there was still the purpose that had brought him to Slaughter Valley—the need to find Ben. He couldn't ride on until that was satisfied.

"What are you expecting him to do?" he asked, leveling his gaze at the merchant.

"I ain't expecting—I'm telling him!" Grissom shot back. "That hardcase bunch from Longhorn'll be coming in here all set to tear things to hell. It's up to him to stop them."

"Alone?"

"You're damned right, alone! It's his problem—same as Max Eagle is his, too, when he shows up looking to square the score for Ward. Like I've said, he don't need to look for help from the town."

"Appears to me he's never had any from the start," Starbuck observed quietly. "This Max Eagle, he live around here?"

"Up Colorado way, but that won't keep him from coming. May not be for a spell, but he'll show, you can bet on that . . . If you had just used your head, Bishop, done what I told you!"

The lawman, taking no part in the largely one-sided conversation, stirred wearily. He was much younger than he first appeared, Shawn realized. He could scarcely be in his mid-twenties. Again he wondered why the man had chosen a job for which he obviously was not fitted.

"Whole thing was a mistake," he murmured.

"Mistake!" Grissom exploded. "It sure was—my hiring you, you bucking Ward, then killing him—all of it! Now there'll be more hell to come."

"You sure you're speaking for the whole town?" Starbuck asked. "Ought to be a few men around here interested in seeing that things are done right. Hard to believe everybody's ready to turn their backs on the marshal."

"That's not how it is. Sure we're willing to stand by him, long as he uses common sense, but he knew same as everybody else knows how things've been with Ward Eagle. We got along with him for years. Marshal ahead of Bishop understood. Strictly left him and his bunch alone. But Bishop here has to go and get all high and mighty and throw a couple of them in jail. That was stupid enough, but then after I calm Ward down by turning them loose, he starts it all over—"

"He never started it," Shawn broke in. "Know that for a fact because I was in the saloon with Eagle and Jack Letterman. Eagle was getting himself drunk, and talking about how he was going to teach the marshal a lesson. Letterman tried to talk him out of it but he wouldn't listen. He was set on making trouble and nobody could stop him."

Grissom chewed at his lower lip. "That's only the

34

way you saw it."

"Ask Rufe Hagerty—and there were three men playing cards. They were in on it, too."

The merchant was silent for a long minute, and then his shoulders moved slightly. "Well, maybe so. Still, if Bishop hadn't started it in the first place—"

"I was only doing what I was hired to do," the lawman muttered. "It's right here in the laws that were wrote up for the town—and nobody told me I was to keep hands off the Longhorn crowd."

"Shouldn't needed telling! Should've had sense enough to know it."

"Just look the other way when Ward Eagle's cowhands, or those of any other rancher who is a good customer of yours and the town's, start tearing things up—that's what it all boils down to, I take it."

At Starbuck's words Henry Grissom's jaw snapped shut. His face darkened. "All right, mister!" he snapped. "You're big at shooting off your mouth about something that's no butt-in of yours. If you feel the marshal's getting the raw end of a deal, then hang around, get him out of the hole he's jockeyed himself into!"

"Might do that," Shawn replied quietly, and moved away from the door as the merchant whirled and started to leave.

"You keep remembering, Bishop!" he shouted over his shoulder. "I'm holding you responsible!"

He reached the door, and in jerking it open, collided with a young woman and a small child just stepping up onto the stoop. Startled, the child went to her knees and began to sob. Grissom, rigid with anger, hurried on.

Shawn moved forward, picked up the small girl as the woman regained her balance, and set her on her feet. He moved to one side, eyes on the woman. She was young, had chestnut-brown hair and calm blue eyes that were soft under their thick, dark lashes. Her skin was smooth ivory, and the stylish dress she wore, strangely out of place here, set off her well-molded figure to perfection.

From inside the office he heard Bishop's voice. "My wife, Carla—and our daughter, Jeannie, Mr.—"

"Starbuck," Shawn supplied, unable to take his gaze off the woman.

She smiled, murmured, "Thank you," and then anxiety claimed her expression as she moved by him into the office. "Arlie—are you all right? I heard there was some kind of trouble—"

"I'm fine," Bishop said, taking the child into his arms and holding her close to quiet her. "But I've Mr. Starbuck to thank for that. He stopped Letterman from shooting me—after I killed Ward Eagle."

The lawman's words seemed almost lightly tossed off. It was clear he was presenting a different front to his wife.

Starbuck glanced at Carla. Her eyes were wide, filled with horror. "You—you killed Ward Eagle?" she gasped.

Abruptly her head sunk, her knees began to buckle, and she swayed forward. Shawn reached out and caught her. The thought, *what kind of people are these?* ran through his mind as he placed her in one of the chairs set against the wall.

* 7*

ARLIE BISHOP HASTILY DEPOSITED his daughter on the edge of the desk, whirled to the bucket standing on a bench in the corner of the room, and scooped up a dipperful of water. Crouching before his wife, he pressed the container to her mouth, forcing a small quantity of the liquid down her throat. Then, wetting his handkerchief, he patted her face gently.

Carla opened her eyes. She stared vaguely about for several moments, before finally settling her eyes upon Bishop. A cry broke from her lips, and throwing her arms about his neck, she broke into tears.

Starbuck, back against the wall, watched in silence. The Bishops were big-city people, he realized, and accustomed to a more civilized life—not to the direct, often brutal ways of the frontier West. They were as out of place in Tannekaw as a Taos mountain man would be on the sidewalks of some great Eastern metropolis.

The lawman rose to his feet and faced Shawn. "My wife—Carla—she's not used to things like this," he explained apologetically. "But she's all right now."

Starbuck nodded, his glance on the woman. Her clean, shining beauty fascinated him. It was as if he were looking at a delicate, exquisitely carved cameo. Helen of Troy, he thought, his mind reverting to those nights long ago when his mother had read to him and Ben of the exploits of the ancient Greeks. She could have been like Carla; certainly, she could not have been more beautiful.

He started, suddenly aware that he was staring, that Carla was smiling at him as she dabbed at her eyes with a square of lace-edged linen.

"I'm sorry," she murmured. "I didn't mean to be such a weakling, but the—"

"Never mind," Arlie said, laying his hand on her shoulder and pressing softly. "Mr. Starbuck—"

"Shawn—"

Bishop smiled, then continued. "Shawn understands. I guess it's hard at first for any woman who moves into this country."

"I feel so foolish. I—I don't think I've ever fainted before, but when you said that you had—"

"No need to talk about it. It's over and done with."

She looked at him earnestly. "Is it? Are you sure?"

The lawman nodded and grasped her by the arm. "I think you and Jeannie had better go home now."

Carla rose to her feet and reached for her daughter's hand. The child slipped off the edge of the desk, placed her small fingers in her mother's, and together they started for the door. Carla paused at the threshold.

"Why don't you bring Shawn to dinner tonight," she said, making it a suggestion rather than a question. "I'm sure he'd enjoy the meal."

Bishop glanced at Starbuck for confirmation.

"Be a pleasure," Shawn said, opening the door.

Carla smiled again, and holding to Jeannie's hand, moved by him into the dwindling sunlight. The crowd in the street had gone, and Starbuck, conscious of the closeness in the small office, allowed the entrance to remain open.

"Want to thank you for stepping in when you did, and stopping Letterman," Bishop said as he went back into the room and settled on one of the chairs. "Would have done so earlier, but I didn't want to go into it in front of my wife. If she knew how near I came to getting myself

38

killed she—well, I don't know what she would do."

The lawman let the words trail off as he sank onto a corner of the desk and stared glumly at the floor.

Starbuck studied him for a bit. Then, "How long've you had this job?"

"Couple of months, almost."

"You don't seem to be fitted for it," Shawn said bluntly.

"Job's a job."

"Not quite. Being a lawman in this country's not the same as being a policeman in some big city back East."

Arlie smiled ruefully. "I'm learning that fast, but I had to take what I could find. Told myself one day that I'd looked into my wife and daughter's eyes and seen hunger tears for the last time—that I was going to find a job that would let me support them right, no matter what it was."

"What did you do before you came here?"

"My father had a furniture factory—in Pennsylvania. Town called Sharpsburg. Not a big plant but it kept busy and it was profitable. I worked in as a sort of errand boy. Wasn't big enough or old enough to do anything else. Then the war came. The factory was hit by artillery shells. My father was killed and the whole place went up in flames. Everything was lost.

"My mother and I went to live with relatives on a farm in Vermont, but times were hard and there just wasn't enough for all of us, so a few years later—I was eighteen—I pulled out, went to New York City. Met Carla there and we got married."

Bishop hesitated, shaking his head. "Worst thing I could have done—for her, I mean. I had only a piecemeal job and never did make enough money to give her even the bare necessities, much less the things that she deserved.

"We finally gave it up, decided to move to the West. It was new country, just opening up, and I heard there were plenty of jobs to be had. Turned out I was wrong. Times were just as hard and jobs just as scarce—at least the kind that I could handle and that paid enough to support a family.

"We knocked about for a few months, with things getting worse and worse, and then word came to me that a town called Tannekaw was looking for a marshal. I asked around and found out where the place was and wrote a letter applying for the job. They hired me and we moved here at once—we'd made it as far west as south Missouri, and I was working as a clerk in a dry-goods store at the time. Was getting paid five dollars a week."

Shawn frowned. "Can't see them hiring you when you didn't have any experience. Takes plenty of that to wear a star."

Arlie Bishop stared at his clenched hands. "That's the mistake I was talking about—I lied. Thought a marshal was the same as the constables I'd seen in the towns where I'd worked—usually old men who served papers and jailed drunks and kept the kids from doing damage on Halloween.

"Found out I was wrong. In fact, I was wrong about everything. Towns out here are different from the ones I was used to. So're the people and their way of living and the way they look at things—their attitude, I—I mean. We've been here two months, like I said, and we haven't made a friend yet, excepting you."

"Expect it's the other way around," Starbuck said. "It's you and your wife who are different. You don't exactly fit in with Western folks. The way your wife

40

dresses, for one thing, if you don't mind my saying it. She's too elegant—too grand, maybe I should say. A thing like that sets her apart."

"No fault of hers. I never could afford to buy her anything to wear. The clothes she's got are the ones she had in New York and brought with her . . . What about me?"

Shawn smiled. "The big city shows through in you, too."

"How? I've tried to be like others around here, and I know there's been a lot of men moving in from the East. Expect you did yourself."

"I know that. Some slide right into the kind of life and habits people out here follow—but some never really do. Far as I'm concerned, I came from Ohio. Learned fast—had to."

"Then there's no reason why I can't," Bishop declared, and then stopped short, a wry expression covering his face. "Not much sense in me figuring on anything in the future, I expect."

"Max Eagle?"

The lawman nodded woodenly. "I lucked out where Ward and Letterman were concerned—thanks to you. Be a different matter when he shows up."

Starbuck was silent, admitting to himself that Arlie Bishop was right.

"I've made a hell of a mess of things. Don't know which is worse—staying back East and starving to death, watching my wife and baby fade away, or coming out here and getting myself killed, leaving them high and dry—to starve."

"Could be it'll work out," Shawn said for lack of something better to say.

Bishop rose, took a nervous turn around the office.

41

"How? Only thing that'll save me would be for Max Eagle to fall off his horse, break his neck—and that's not liable to happen."

"Man never knows. About all he can do is take things as they come and do what he can to get ready."

Bishop halted. "Get ready? Not much I can do along those lines. Trying to match myself with a gunfighter would be stupid—silly. He'd kill me before I could reach for my pistol."

"You've got a brain—use it. Outsmart him."

"How? What could I do?"

Starbuck's shoulders shrugged. "Got no answer for that. Meanwhile, let it ride. You could get lucky."

"Not me," Bishop said heavily. "Luck and me are total strangers."

He glanced to the street and picked up his hat. "Getting dark. Expect Carla's about got din—supper ready," he said, and then forced a smile. "Condemned man's entitled to eat a hearty meal. Reckon that applies to me."

* 8*

THE HOUSE WHERE THE BISHOPS LIVED was a hundred
yards or so in back of the jail. It was a small, square,
peaked-roof structure, once white but now bleached to
gray by the seasons. It had a comfortable appearance,
however, squatting as it did between two large
cottonwood trees, with a garden running along the south
side, a chicken yard and cowpen to the rear, and a
scatter of aging, friendly sheds to the north of the open
yard that lay behind.

In the last flush of sunlight, now spreading a warm
amber haze over the land, all things were soft-edged and
hushed, and as they crossed the intervening vacant lots
to the sagging rail fence fronting the place, Arlie Bishop
sighed.

"We could be happy here," he said pensively. "It's all
we've ever wanted. Sure wish it had worked out."

"Don't give up on it yet," Starbuck replied.

Bishop again musteredd a forced smile. "Still figuring
Max Eagle will fall off his horse?"

"Never know," Shawn said, and followed the lawman
up a narrow path to the house.

Bishop opened the door to the good smells of cooking
food and the gentle glow of lighted lamps. He led him
through a scantily furnished parlor into an adjoining
room, where a square table, covered by a snowwhite
cloth, had been set for the meal.

Carla appeared in a connecting doorway at that
moment, cool and charming in a pale-blue, close-fitting
dress, across the waist of which she wore a
lacetrimmed, embroidered apron. She had pulled her

43

hair to the top of her head and had fastened it in place with a bit of ribbon. In the mellow light it looked almost black.

"I'm so glad you came," she said formally, her eyes warm and friendly.

Starbuck nodded, and felt the old longing within him stir—a place of his own, a wife like Carla waiting for him—but it was a far-off dream, one not likely to come true soon. And, too, he doubted if he would ever again encounter a woman like her. There could not be another to match the quiet, complete beauty of Carla Bishop.

"Everything is ready," she said, holding her arms wide, palms open, to include the table. "Sit down and I'll serve."

Arlie caught at her hand, stayed her. "You all right now?"

"I'm fine," she said and turned away.

Bishop faced Shawn, pointed to a chair and selected one for himself. Carla appeared in the doorway carrying a platter on which was heaped mashed potatoes and sliced roast beef. She made return trips to the kitchen to bring bowls of vegetables, plates of hot biscuits, fresh butter, and honey.

"We'll have our coffee last," she said, finally taking her place.

It was a meal such as Starbuck had not sat down to in years, and when it was over, and Carla produced wedges of savory apple pie to top it off, he found himself unable to finish the dessert, despite his liking for it.

"Should have saved a little room," he said, apologetically.

Carla beamed. "I love to see a man eat a big meal. It tells me that he is enjoying it. . . . Shall we have our coffee in the parlor?"

She pushed back from the table, bringing Shawn and Bishop to their feet. They returned to the front room, halted there, waiting until Carla appeared with an ebony tray, upon which were a silver pot and three cups and saucers. She motioned them to be seated, and after serving them, settled down on the worn couch placed against an inside wall.

It was all very sedate, reminding Starbuck of Sunday afternoons on the farm in Muskingum when the minister and his wife would drop by.

"Jeannie asleep?" Arlie asked, breaking the silence. Carla nodded. "She was tired—wanted to wait up for you but just couldn't."

"I'll look in on her before I leave," he said, and set his empty cup on the tray. "Right now I'd better see to my chores."

Shawn started to rise. "I'll give you a hand—"

The lawman waved him back. "Stay right there, keep Carla company—and have some more coffee. I won't be long."

Starbuck eased back into the rocker. Carla leaned forward and refilled his cup. Without raising her eyes she said, "Was there more trouble after I left?"

There was a small, red jewel in the center of the clasp that held the ribbon in her hair, he noted, and the flawless skin along the curving edge of her lowcut dress, where her breasts pushed upward, was still white, unbronzed by the sun.

"No—none," he said.

She sighed, returning the pot to its tray. "I'm afraid for Arlie—for all of us, I guess. He could have been killed today if it hadn't been for you, and now, with this—this gunfighter coming—"

45

Starbuck's eyes narrowed. "You know about that?"
"Overheard it on the street. People were talking about it."

"He didn't want you to know."

Carla brushed at her cheek, pushing back a wisp of hair that had freed itself. "He's that way—always trying to keep the bad things from me. He's not very good at it, the same as he's not good at anything."

"Seems to me he's tried."

"Oh, I'm not saying he hasn't. He just never learned a trade or a profession. His folks were well-to-do, and there was no need for it as long as there was the furniture company. They expected him to take over one day, I guess. When it was lost, everything went wrong for him."

She was holding tight to herself, Starbuck realized as he listened to her low, near hopeless voice. The slightest thing would cause the dam to burst, and he quickly sought to direct her mind into another channel.

"You've made a fine home here."

She smiled. "I didn't have much to work with, only a few things that belonged to my family and that I held on to. It's comfortable and we have about everything we need. Arlie bought us a cow and some chickens out of his first month's pay, and our garden is coming along. We have plenty to eat now . . . Do you think there's any hope—for him, I mean, when this gunfighter gets here?"

Starbuck stirred uncomfortably under the direct question. "He'll find a way out."

"But he can't possibly face a man like that an experienced killer!"

"There'll be some way to handle it. Something will turn up—tomorrow is always a better day."

Carla shook her head. "I'm tired of looking for

46

tomorrows. It seems that's all I've ever done—all of my life. Now, with this terrible thing coming, I'm afraid—afraid for Arlie and for what will become of Jeannie and me."

"It'll come out all right," Starbuck assured her, still endeavoring to divert her dark thoughts. He glanced around. "I once lived in a home like this—far away from here."

Carla straightened slowly and smiled. "I imagined you came from somewhere else. You don't talk or act like most people here. Where was your home?"

"Ohio. Farm on the Muskingum River. Expect I sound a little different from the others because my mother was a schoolteacher. She taught my brother and me—along with the regular schooling she insisted we get."

"Did she give you the name Shawn?"

Starbuck nodded. "Comes from Shawnee. They were a tribe of Indians she worked among. Liked the sound of the word, I guess."

"It's unusual." Carla locked her hands in her lap and studied them. "Oh, I wish we could move—go back home! Anywhere in the East, I wouldn't care. I can't get used to this land. And people are so hard and cold."

"Find them there, too. It's just a matter of making friends."

"How? We've tried, but you're the only person we've met since we came to this town who showed any interest. Everyone else avoids us. I thought we'd be welcome, but they'll have nothing to do with us."

He'd gone over the same road only an hour or so earlier with Arlie, but recognizing the quiet desperation that gripped her, Starbuck said, patiently, "You're not like them, and I don't think they know just how to take

47

you. Makes them standoffish."

"You mean we're different? How?"

"The way you dress, for one thing—not that there's anything wrong with it. It's a treat for any man to see a woman in an expensive, beautiful gown such as you wear, but they don't go with this country."

"They're all I have except for some old things—"

"You're better off using them, at least for a while. You need to sort of work up to an outfit like you have on now. Be a good idea to wait until there's a barn dance or maybe a church social. Women around here can't understand your wearing it around the house or on the street."

"But I like to dress up around the house. I do it for Arlie."

"I can appreciate that. Like to think that someday I'll have a wife who'll feel the same way, but you've got to remember that these folks have had it hard, and they can't forget it. Makes them sort of resent people who look as if they've had it easier. Human nature, I guess.

"And something else—serving coffee in your parlor like this. Here everybody sits around the kitchen table and takes their coffee from the pot. Serving it in silver is fine for special occasions—a wedding or maybe a funeral—but doing it every day makes them think you're high-toned. Using the same pot it's made in gives them the idea you want them to feel at home."

Carla toyed with the lace edge of her apron. "I don't see why I should change. It's the way I was brought up."

"I don't blame you, and far as I'm concerned you shouldn't have to change. This country needs sprucing up, but it's a little raw yet, and young. If you're going to live in it, you'll have to join it first. Once you've become a part of it, then's the time to start polishing. Others will accept the idea and be all for it."

She made no reply for a long minute, seemingly lost in the contemplation of his words. Abruptly her slight shoulders twitched.

"It makes no difference anyway—not with what's ahead for Arlie. There's no future here for him or for Jeannie and me."

"Best not to look at it that way. Just hope—"

"I'm tired of hoping, too, and—"

She checked her words as a door at the rear of the house opened, then closed quietly. A moment later Bishop entered the room.

"All done," he said cheerfully. "Cow's fed, chickens are cooped, and I brought up some kindling and fire wood for the stove. You two get a lot of talking out of the way?"

Carla smiled. "Shawn was telling me about his home in Ohio."

"So he said. Can sure tell he wasn't born in this part of the country. . . . Expect we'd best be getting back to the office."

Shawn came upright as Carla, frowning, got to her feet quickly. "Do you have to be there tonight? I thought—"

"Few things I need to do," the lawman said, putting his arm around her. "Could be a bit late, so don't wait up for me."

Shawn moved to the door, halted, and broke the sudden hush that fell between the two. "Want to thank you again for the fine dinner. Can't remember when I enjoyed one so much."

Carla recovered herself, and managed a smile. "I hope you'll come again—and thank you for a pleasant

49

evening."

Starbuck stepped out into the warm night, waiting until Bishop was beside him. He felt the lawman's fingers bite into his arm.

"She knows, doesn't she—about Max Eagle?"

Shawn nodded. "Heard folks talking about it. I tried to reassure her."

"Not much chance of that," Bishop said in a toneless voice. "She knows me too well."

9

THE LAMPS IN THE STORES ALONG THE STREET were burning brightly when they reached the jail, filling the separating area between the buildings with a soft radiance. Quite a few persons were moving along on the sidewalks, and Starbuck could see a goodly number in the various buildings performing their shopping chores. Established customs were hard to break; even at this time of the year, patrons preferred to search out their needs in the coolness of the evening, just as they did during the summer months when the heat was intense.

Shawn stood for a bit, idly listening to the ragged music filtering through the hub-bub within the Valley Queen and drifting into the night, while his glance ran the length of the double row of structures. He could see Henry Grissom in his establishment nearby, talking with Hagerty and two other men.

"Who's that with the mayor?" he asked.

Bishop swung his attention to the general store. "Sol Wiseman's the one in the middle. That's Billy Smith on the left. Hagerty you know. Why?"

"Let's have a little talk with them. Grissom's had time to cool off. May be looking at things different now."

"About me, you mean?"

"You and the Longhorn crowd. Expect they'll be showing up pretty soon."

The lawman swore quietly. "Thinking about Max Eagle—I'd forgot all about them."

"Then you've got it backward. They'll come first, and that puts them at the head of the list. Eagle will be here

51

later—tomorrow, the next day, or a week from now. We'll think about him after we get by Longhorn."

"*We?*" Bishop repeated in a tense voice. "Does that mean you're aiming to help me—do what Grissom said?"

"Expect to be around for a few days asking about my brother. I'll do what I can."

Starbuck moved on, and with Arlie Bishop at his side, mounted the steps to the porch of the store. Grissom and the men with him ceased their conversing when they entered, and turned to face them.

"If you've come here looking for help," the merchant said before either could speak, "you're wearing out shoe leather. We ain't having nothing to do—"

"It's your town," Shawn cut in. "Ought to be plenty hard for you to look at things that way."

"Not the town that bunch'll be after—it's him. If we don't interfere, they'll leave us alone."

"Maybe. Bishop represents the town—all of you."

"Not much he does and they know that! Made that clear earlier. Things were going along fine, no trouble at all to speak of until he started throwing his weight around. Now he can just take the consequences."

Starbuck glanced at Hagerty and the other men. "That the way you all feel about it?"

The saloon owner looked away. Billy Smith shrugged. Only Wiseman spoke. "Henry's the mayor. We go by what he thinks is right."

"Not much right in turning down a man who's only trying to do a job for you."

"We wouldn't be backing off if he'd listened to me," Grissom declared angrily. "He knew better'n to cross Ward."

"Maybe. Seems to me, however, you should've given

52

him the names of your special friends—the ones you didn't want him to arrest when he took the job," Shawn said drily. "If he'd wanted to be that kind of a lawman, then he could've avoided this."

"Figured he'd know enough to use his head," the mayor retorted. "A good marshal would've—"

"A good marshal would've done just what Bishop did or he would've thrown that star right back in your face—which is what Bishop ought to do!"

Starbuck saw Arlie stiffen, frown as worry clouded his eyes.

"Then why don't he? Might save us all a lot of grief."

"Mainly because he thinks too much of the job and the responsibilities he swore to uphold. You don't deserve a good lawman—"

"Lawman! Ain't sure he is one—or ever was!"

"Little late to wonder about it. You hired him, and he figures to stand by his word. If you want to fire him, have him leave this town cold naked, that's up to you. The Longhorn crowd would like that fine, along with the rest of the hardcases in the valley, I expect."

Grissom's brow knitted. He tugged at the front of his bib apron nervously, glancing at the men grouped around him.

"Nobody said anything about firing. Where'd you get that idea?" he added, turning to the marshal.

Bishop swallowed hard. "Way you've been talking—the things you said—"

Starbuck threw an impatient look at the man. If he would only stand up for himself—show a little fire, a bit of backbone! He had bluffed his way into the job, now he needed to continue the counterfeit, make it appear he was capable of wearing the star.

"Well, I won't say I ain't considering it," Grissom

stated, again in control of the situation. "And I don't mind telling you here and now I'm liable to make a change unless things straighten out."

"Meaning what?" Starbuck asked, drawing attention away from Bishop, who was standing aside, head down, like a schoolboy caught with his hand in the candy jar.

"Well, the Longhorn bunch, for one thing. I figure they're only coming in to hooraw him. If he keeps it that way so's they won't tear up the town—"

"You saying he's to just let them rag him around, do what they want?" Shawn asked, incredulously.

"That's it," Grissom said flatly. "He asked for a licking—up to him to take it."

"You any idea what that would do to the meaning of the law?"

"Ain't worried about that, only about keeping my town from getting wrecked."

Starbuck shrugged in disbelief. "The same goes for Max Eagle, I reckon."

"It does. That's up to him, too. Best thing I can think of is for him to meet the man, tell him it was all a mistake—an accident, maybe—and ask him friendly like if he won't let it ride."

"Crawl—"

"About what it amounts to. Way I see it, it's either that or shoot it out with Max, and everybody knows how that'll end."

"I see," Shawn murmured. He turned to Arlie Bishop. "Guess we've got the picture. Mayor wants you to be the whipping boy for that Longhorn crowd. Then if you've learned your lesson after they're through with you, and if you're willing to get down on your belly in the dust and kiss Max Eagle's boots, he'll think about letting you keep your badge. You want to stick around

54

on those terms?"

The lawman did not look up. "Ain't much else I can do," he murmured.

Billy Smith scratched at the growth on his chin. "We can take that two ways. You staying because you ain't got nowheres else to go or because you're too proud to run?"

"Because he aims to show you that you're wrong," Shawn replied. "This place needs law and order, same as all towns do, and he wants to give it to you."

"Not at the expense of having the place all tore to hell!" Grissom warned.

"Expect whatever happens, will happen," Starbuck said. "If you're afraid of hurting somebody's feelings, stay out of sight when Longhorn shows up. That'll give them the idea you don't know anything about it . . . Come on, Marshal."

Wheeling, Shawn headed for the door, Bishop a step behind him. They paused as Grissom's voice reached out to them.

"Mind you, now—there'd better not be no damage!"

"If there is," Starbuck said coldly, "you can blame yourself for hamstringing the law in the beginning."

10

"AFRAID YOU DID A LOT of BIG TALKING IN THERE," Bishop said hesitantly as they moved off the store's landing and stepped down to the level of the street. "Ain't sure I—"

"About time you started doing a little talking for yourself!" Starbuck snapped impatiently. "Hell, man, you wanted this job—and you need it. Face up to your own bargain."

"But I can't—"

"The hell you can't! Maybe you're no top hand as a lawman, but you can make a showing. You've got to start acting and looking like a marshal. Walk straight, speak up loud when you're talking, whether or not it means much of anything. Quit hanging your head in front of Grissom and the others. They pull on their pants a leg at a time same as you do."

Irritability still possessed Starbuck when they reached the jail and entered. Bishop struck a match to the lamp on his desk and set the wick and chimney. His features were strained as he slowly came about.

"All right for you to speak out the way you did. But me—I can't back up what I say—"

"No reason why you can't—up to a point!" Shawn replied brusquely. "Believe a little in yourself and quit down-grading your chances."

"Easy for you to say that, too. Me—I just never been able to do anything right that's worth a damn."

"Well, I guess you could say the time's come," Starbuck said, glancing around the office. "I'm going to see to it."

A fleeting expression of relief crossed Arlie Bishop's face, changing as quickly to puzzlement. "Been thinking about what you said earlier—about helping me. And now going through all this. Set me to wondering why."

"Do I need a reason?"

"Seems to me you would, taking on my load the way you are, making an enemy of Jack Letterman and the rest of Longhorn."

"No sweat there. Made a few before this."

"But going out of your way—not that I don't appreciate it, understand—but it seems sort of strange."

Shawn turned to a second lamp bracketed on the wall and touched a match to its black-edged wick, increasing the illumination in the room.

"Let's just say that I figured you need a little help, and that maybe I don't like to see that star you're wearing and what it stands for kicked around."

His words stopped there. He could have added he felt Carla deserved more, that she and their small daughter deserved a better life than the one they had so far been subjected to, but he let it pass. Arlie Bishop had some pride left.

"Best we start thinking a little about Longhorn."

The lawman sank into his chair disconsolately. "Could be we ought to just let them have their way. They won't kill me, that's for sure. Got to save me for that gunfighter."

"I'll listen to no talk like that!" Shawn said curtly. "I'm not about to give them the satisfaction of roasting the law, so forget it. You're going to show them and this whole damned town that you're the marshal, and that the star you're wearing means something."

"How? I don't know what to do, where to begin."

"First off, like I've already said, you're to start acting

57

like a lawman. Think a little, use your brain. It was a fool stunt you pulled using a single-barreled gun on Ward Eagle. Gave you one shot, then—you were through—finished. If you had been thinking, you would've grabbed up a double-barrel, provided yourself with a little edge."

"I had a single-shot like that when I was a boy. Used it to go rabbit hunting. Reckon that's why I picked it— and I wasn't thinking about a second shot. I can see now that was foolish."

"It's in the past—done with. Just begin using your head, because those are the kind of mistakes that get you killed. A six gun's better for a lawman, anyway."

"I've never used one—hardly know how."

"Wear one just the same, and learn to handle it. Meanwhile, carry a double-barreled scattergun, too, if it feels better to you. . . . Now, next thing is figure out what kind of a welcome party we can give Letterman and his bunch. Heard you say something about the town ordinances. Do you remember if there was a law against a man carrying a gun?"

Arlie lowered his gaze stared thoughtfully at the floor. The music in the Valley Queen had risen to a higher level and was now being accompanied by a rhythmic stomping of boots.

"Seems I recollect there was," he said, and pulled open the top drawer of the desk. "Can mighty quick tell."

He rummaged about in the papers, old envelopes, and stacks of wanted posters filling the compartment, finally producing a sheaf of handwritten sheets held together with grocer's twine. "Here's a copy of the laws I found when I took over," he said, laying the stack before him and thumbing through it. Abruptly he stopped. "Yeh, here it is: *It shall be unlawful for anyone to carry firearms within the limits of the town."*

"All we have to know," Starbuck said. "We'll need a couple of signs. Seen any around?"

Bishop shook his head. "Cleared out the place good when I moved in. Weren't any signs—probably because the law's never been enforced."

"No problem. We can make them. Dig out a couple of those wanted posters—the cardboard kind. I'll use the back side."

Arlie quickly selected two of the oblong notices, and laid them on the desk. Shawn, finding nothing else suitable with which to write, thumbed a bullet from his belt, and bending over the cards, printed in block letters as large as he could manage:

UNLAWFUL TO CARRY GUNS INSIDE TOWN LIMITS
A. Bishop, Town Marshal

"Sign it," he said when he had completed the first, and sliding it to the lawman, prepared the second with identical wording.

"Be needing some nails or tacks," he said when Bishop had affixed his signature.

"Got them, all right. Use them for putting up posters," Arlie said, taking a small brown sack from the drawer. He dropped it on the desk and pointed at the signs. "What are we going to do with these?"

"Post them—one at each end of town."

"Why?" Bishop wondered, still not understanding.

"You've got to have something to stand on when you go up against Longhorn. This gives you your authority."

Arlie nodded slowly. "Think I see what you mean. Fixes it so's I can arrest any man wearing a gun, but mostly Jack Letterman and his bunch."

59

"Right. It's them you're interested in. Covers everybody else, too, being a town law. And since you're the marshal, you're obliged to enforce it."

Bishop rose to his feet, his features going taut. "You're carrying me a little fast," he said doubtfully. "I ain't sure I know—"

"It's simple. Letterman and his friends will show up, all packing guns. There's a town ordinance against it. You'll arrest the lot of them, throw them in jail. By doing that you'll beat them to the punch."

Bishop looked at him in amazement. "*Me*—arrest them?"

"You're the marshal, aren't you?—and they'll be breaking the law. I'll side you as a sort of deputy."

A measure of relief filtered into Arlie's eyes. "Makes it different. I don't quite see why we're doing it, however."

"A way of letting them know that you're the town marshal and you mean business."

"What about Grissom? He said—"

"The hell with him!" Starbuck said, wearily patient. "Quit worrying about him and what he said. Talk never yet drew blood—and you'll only be doing the job you were hired to do. It's their law—and nobody can say it shouldn't be enforced. Come on, let's get those notices up."

Bishop took the two cards in one hand, the tacks in the other. "These're pretty small. Doubt if they'll be seen."

"Make no difference. Being there does," Shawn said and wheeled to the gun rack mounted against the wall. Selecting a sawed-off, double-barreled shotgun from the half dozen weapons, he tripped it open, made certain it was loaded. Satisfied, he snapped it shut, and taking the cards from Arlie, handed it to him.

"From now on you carry this under your arm every

60

time you step out of this office. Anybody sees you, they're going to see that scattergun, too."

A half smile, hard at the corners, pulled at Bishop's mouth. Hooking the weapon's stock under his right armpit and bracing it on his wrist, he followed Shawn into the open.

They paused on the landing. A light wind had sprung up, cool with the reminder that winter had not as yet fully relinquished its grip on the land. There were fewer people abroad than earlier, but the lamps in the stores were still bright, laying their patches of yellow light across the roadway.

"Walk down the middle," Starbuck said. "It's a good habit. A man can see better, and it makes it easy to spot someone standing in one of the passageways or at the corner of a building."

Bishop made no comment, stepping out to the center of the street, and shoulder to shoulder they marched to its lower end, where the ruts entering from the west intersected. Selecting one of the cottonwoods that stood on the corner, they tacked the notice to its trunk, reversed themselves, and back-tracked to the opposite end of the town, where they affixed the second sign to a post near the Silver Dollar Saloon.

"Now you've declared yourself," Starbuck said as they started the return to the jail. "Just hope Grissom doesn't take it on himself to tear them down before Longhorn gets here."

"Everybody was watching, seemed," Arlie said, a note of pride in his voice. "Didn't see Grissom in his store, however . . . What if he does?"

"We put them back up," Shawn replied. "Thing for you to keep remembering is that you're the marshal, not him."

61

11

ONCE AGAIN IN THE LAWMAN'S office, Shawn stepped into the room in which the cells stood. Lighting the single lamp hanging on the wall, he examined the barred doors of the twin cages. Both were locked. He turned to Bishop.

"Open them up and leave them ajar. There have been a good many prisoners making an escape while a lawman fussed with a stuck lock."

Arlie moved by him, a ring of keys jangling in his hand, and released the cross-hatched iron panels. "You figure we'll have to use them both?" he asked as they returned to the office area.

Choosing a chair near the window, Starbuck sat down. "Depends on how many come in with Letterman—and whether they pay any attention to the signs or not. Don't be afraid to jam them in there tight. Jail's not supposed to be a comfortable place."

Bishop hung the keys on the peg provided for them behind his desk and sank into its chair. Frowning, he glanced to the street. "Could be they won't show up."

"Possible," Shawn admitted, but he doubted it very much. Jack Letterman, heir apparent to the leadership of Longhorn's hardcase faction, could hardly afford to pass up administering a lesson of vengeance calculated to establish also his status in the town.

Almost immediately the dust-muffled thud of horses entering the street reached him. Bishop caught the sound, too, and as Starbuck rose and stepped into the doorway, he came to his feet hastily, snatching up the shotgun propped against the wall, and crossed to the entrance.

"That them?" he asked in a tight voice.

"Letterman—and six riders," Shawn answered, eyes on the men as they swung into the hitchrack fronting the Valley Queen. "All armed."

The lawman drew a deep breath and turned his glance to Starbuck. "Then I guess we'd better—"

"Not yet. Let them get inside." Shawn studied Bishop narrowly. "Ease off."

Arlie wiped nervously at the sweat suddenly beading his forehead. "Not sure I can go through with this . . . Six . . . seven of them, only two of us. I—"

"No problem. That star you're wearing counts for something."

Bishop ran a shaky hand over his chin. "What if they refuse—put up a fight?"

"They won't."

"But what if they do?"

"We'll both be carrying guns. We'll use them."

Bishop seemed to wilt. He leaned against the door frame and wagged his head. "Not sure I can."

"That doesn't make sense. You pulled the trigger on Ward Eagle."

"That was different, somehow. He was drawing his pistol to shoot me. I did it sort of without thinking."

"Be the same—only they won't try it. Nobody's anxious to die, and looking at the muzzle of a shotgun does something to a man. Those two holes seem as big as silver dollars."

Bishop was not listening. "I was a fool," he muttered. "Should've never taken the job—"

"But you did, and this is a part of it!" Shawn snapped, impatient once again with the man. "No choice now, anyway. You can't run, not even if you wanted to. Letterman wouldn't let you. There's one thing left; go

63

through with it, and get in the first lick."

Arlie sighed. "Reckon you're right." He glanced toward the saloon, opposite and a short distance down the street. The riders were inside. He drew himself up stiffly. "I'm ready."

Relief slipped through Starbuck. For a long breath he had thought Bishop was going to cave in on him and back out. He appeared now to have a grip on himself.

"Let's go," he said, and ducked his head at the weapon in the lawman's hand. "That loaded?"

Bishop shrugged. "Guess so," he said, and tripped the barrel release to check.

"Don't ever guess. It's another mistake that could cost you your life. Look every time you pick it up, then you'll know."

"It's loaded," Arlie said woodenly, and stepped out onto the landing.

"Remember, walk in the middle of the street," Shawn said, throwing his gaze up and down the sidewalks. "You want everybody to see this—and when we get inside, do the talking. I'm just a deputy."

Bishop nodded tautly. "Sure, sure," he said in a strained voice.

They traveled the short distance to the saloon, crossed the porch to the batwing doors, then halted. A steady din of conversation, punctuated by an occasional laugh, was coming from the well-lighted interior.

Starbuck put his hand on the swinging panel on his side to push it open, waiting for Bishop to do likewise. The lawman's face was white, his lips tightly compressed. A brightness filled his eyes. A tremor of misgiving raced through Starbuck. He wasn't out of the woods yet; Arlie Bishop could still fail, could back down at the last moment and leave the chore to him.

His mouth drew into a hard-set grin. He'd asked for it—butting in where he had no call to. He should have stayed clear of the whole mess, just as he'd promised himself he'd do, instead getting soft-hearted, wading in and taking it upon himself to turn a greenhorn into a lawman. By God, if it wasn't for Carla—

He shook off the thought of dropping the whole thing right there, reached out with his free hand, and pressed Bishop's arm reassuringly.

"Ready?"

Arlie swallowed hard, then nodded.

"All right, let's move in . . . Don't forget—you're the law."

12

THEY STEPPED THROUGH the Valley Queen's entrance together and halted just within. Starbuck instantly swept the depths of the saloon with a sharp, assessing glance.

Letterman and his Longhorn followers were at the bar; two dozen or so other patrons were at the tables scattered about the room. There was a gaudily dressed woman at the piano, while three or four others, similarly clad, were moving about in the crowd. Rufe Hagerty, in a business suit, and a balding, black-mustached man wearing an apron, stood behind the counter.

The rumble of talk diminished gradually as eyes turned toward the batwings. Shortly it died entirely, along with the phlegmatic efforts of the pianist. Hagerty looked up from some scribbling he was doing in a small book and frowned. At that same moment, Jack Letterman and the men with him, suddenly aware of the hush, wheeled to see the cause of the distraction.

Longhorn's foreman eased back against the bar gently, hooking his elbows on its edge. Lips curling, he said something aside to his friends. All laughed, and a big red-headed bull of a man, standing well over six feet in height and undoubtedly tipping the scales at no less than two hundred and fifty pounds, nodded and rubbed his clublike hands together.

"Let's finish it," Shawn murmured, and started forward.

Bishop, grim, features taut as stretched cowhide, swung the shotgun he carried under his arm to where it was gripped by both hands in front of him, and fell into step with Starbuck. The silence in the Valley Queen was absolute as they drew up before the men at the bar.

Shawn waited, poised, eyes fixed on Letterman but taking in the other punchers as well. The heavy quiet continued. He resisted the urge to shift his attention to Bishop. Why the hell didn't Arlie speak up, say the words they'd rehearsed? Every second that ticked by was reducing the impact of their approach and increasing the probability of violence.

"Now, what've we got here?" Letterman drawled.

Starbuck cursed inwardly. Bishop had fumbled it, had feathered out at the last moment. The fingers of his left hand, hovering near the butt of his low-slung pistol, spread slowly.

"This here's the marshal, Red," Letterman continued in the same bantering tone to the big man at his side. "He's the one. We're aiming to pull down his britches and let you give him a right good paddling so's—"

"You're all under arrest!" Bishop shouted in a sudden gust of words.

Jack Letterman's brows lifted as his mouth gaped. He smiled. "Arrest? Now, just what kind of a game are you playing?"

"No game," Arlie replied, seemingly taking courage from the sound of his own voice. "Mean what I said."

One of the riders cocked his hat to the back of his head. "Arresting us for what?"

"Carrying firearms inside the town. There's a law—"

"The hell there is! Where'd it come from?"

"It's in the town ordinances."

"Well, I sure never heard of it," Letterman said indifferently.

"Signs posted at both ends of the street."

"We didn't see no signs," another of the punchers grumbled.

67

"No fault of mine. They're there."

Longhorn's foreman was studying Bishop intently. "You ain't loco enough to think you can jug us on a damn fool thing like that, are you?"

"It's the law and I'm enforcing it. You're all going to jail."

"The hell we are—"

"You heard the marshal!" Starbuck cut in harshly, taking a step forward. "You're all under arrest. Start shucking those gunbelts—now!"

None of the Longhorn crew stirred. Starbuck's arm moved slightly. His hand came up. Lamplight glinted dully on the pistol he was holding. The riders, moving only their heads, glanced uncertainly at Jack Letterman. He continued to stare at Bishop, providing them with no answer.

Abruptly, the man at the end of the line shrugged, reached slowly for the buckle of his belt, tripped the tongue, and permitted the thick leather band with its row of brass cartridges and holstered pistol to fall to the floor.

"All of you—move!" Starbuck snarled.

From the corner of his eye he saw Bishop close in, the tall hammers of the old scattergun drawn back to full cock. *Not too near!* he warned silently. One of the hardcases, suspecting the lawman's inexperience and tempted to gamble, could make a grab for the barrel of the weapon. Something like that might set off a whirlwind of death. But Arlie remained cautious, kept out of reach.

One by one the riders dropped their belted weapons. Letterman alone stood motionless, defiant.

"Means you, too!" Starbuck snapped, and stepping forward, pressed the muzzle of his forty-five into the

68

man's belly.

Jack Letterman's hard gaze lowered. He shrugged, released his gear and allowed it to fall in a pile at his feet.

"Now, turn around lay your hands flat on the bar," Shawn ordered, pulling away a half stride.

The Longhorn men complied reluctantly, their boots making a shuffling sound in the tense hush as they came about. Shawn motioned at Bishop to keep them covered, and holstering his own weapon, began to collect the belts and place them in a heap at the end of the bar, well beyond any of the riders' reach.

Nodding to Hagerty, he said, "Be back for these later," then wheeled to Letterman and the other Longhorn men. "All right, let's go. We're taking a walk to the jail. First one of you to try something cute gets hurt. That clear?"

There was no reply from the men as they pivoted and sullenly started for the swinging doors. Arlie, shotgun leveled, stepped in behind and slightly to the side of the closely bunched party. Starbuck assumed a like position opposite.

They reached the porch, moved down into the street, and slanted for the jail. There was no bravado, no derisive humor evident among the Longhorn riders now, only a sour submission and rankling embarrassment. Shawn glanced at the lawman. Arlie was walking ramrod straight, still in the grip of tension. It was not possible to tell if the taste of victory had strengthened him or not.

"Hold on there!"

At the command Starbuck and the others slowed, coming to a halt at the sight of Henry Grissom running toward them. The merchant, face ruddy with anger, eyes snapping, stopped in front of Bishop.

"What's the meaning of this?" he demanded breathlessly.

"Arrested them . . . for carrying firearms inside the town limits."

"You what?" Grissom cried in a strangled, disbelieving voice. "What kind of a fool stunt is this? Every man wears a gun around here."

"There's a law against it."

"I don't give a damn if there is. You turn these men loose—right now!"

Arlie Bishop faltered. "Well I—"

"Back off, Grissom," Starbuck warned coldly. "You're interfering with a lawman doing his job."

"Goddammit, it ain't his job to go around arresting folks for doing nothing!"

"Doesn't apply to this bunch. It's a known fact they were coming in to make trouble. The marshal simply made use of a town ordinance that forbids the carrying of guns to stop them. Signs were posted earlier. They ignored them—and they're going to jail for it."

"The hell they are!" Grissom yelled, thoroughly beside himself. He spun to face Bishop. "Turn them loose! I'm ordering—"

"You're asking to get jailed, too—for interfering," Shawn said warningly. "Law against that."

"Me? You can't jail me! I'm the mayor."

"And Bishop's the marshal, with authority to arrest anybody who bucks the law—which you're doing. Move on," he added, prodding the man nearest him with the barrel of his pistol.

Letterman and the others resumed their slow progress toward the jail. People along the street had become aware of the startling incident unfolding before them in

70

the glow of lamplight, either having noted it by chance or attracted to it by Henry Grissom's infuriated voice, and a growing crowd was congregating in front of the Far West Hotel

The small, tight cavalcade reached the jail's hitchrack, then slowed. In carefully lowered tones Letterman said something to the men flanking him. Abruptly they all halted.

"Keep going!" Starbuck barked, senses alert.

Jack Letterman shook his head. "We ain't walking in there and getting ourselves locked up. You'll plain have to take us."

"No problem," Shawn said mildly, and clubbed the rider nearest him solidly above the ear.

The man howled, went to his knees. Starbuck smiled at the Longhorn foreman sardonically. "That tell you anything, mister?"

Letterman only stared at the fallen rider, watching him get back to his feet laboriously. Red, standing near him, swore, and spat contemptuously into the dust.

"You're a plumb big man with that iron in your hand, deputy. I'm wondering how little you'd be without it."

"Yeh," one of the riders chimed in. "Jasper toting a badge and holding a gun sure does figure he's the top cock. If it wasn't for them guns, your law wouldn't amount to nothing—not a damn nothing!"

"Just what I'm telling you," Red said. "Take away them irons and they'll hightail it like scared rabbits."

Shawn's cool gaze touched the sly, expectant faces of the men. They were goading Bishop and him, he realised, hoping to salvage their badly defaced image. A stubbornness filled him. Since he was out to prove the character and strength of the law, he might as well go all the way, pretend to fall into their trap, and trust he could

71

vanquish the detractors.

He chose big Red, since it was apparent Letterman had brought him along specifically for the purpose of chastising the marshal.

"Maybe you'd like to try backing that up," he, said quietly.

13

RED GRINNED, exposing his broad, yellowed teeth. "You meaning me?"

"You're the one doing all the loud talking."

"Yes, Sir, I sure am!"

Shawn glanced at Arlie Bishop. The lawman was frozen, not certain what he should do. Beyond him the crowd, sensing more excitement, was edging in closer. He wondered, vaguely, what had become of Henry Grissom. He was no longer present.

"Make you a deal, friend," Jack Letterman said, smiling. "You fight Red and beat him, and we'll put ourselves in your jail and stay there nice and quiet 'til the marshal's ready to let us out. He wallops you, we go free now."

A murmur ran through the onlookers. Starbuck shook his head. "You know better than that. The law makes no deals. You're all under arrest, and you get locked up no matter how it comes out."

"Could be that by the time Red's done you won't be in no shape to do nothing."

Starbuck looked again at Bishop. The same thought was running through the lawman's mind, he guessed . . . He'd have to gamble once more—for Arlie's sake.

"Doubt it. Long as the marshal's holding that shotgun you'll do what he says. Now, you and the rest of your bunch line up there against the front of the jail, where he can watch you."

Red licked his lips expectantly. "That mean me and you're going to fight?" he asked as the remaining

Longhorn men moved toward the low building.

"That's what you said you wanted," Shawn said crisply. He nodded to Bishop. "Don't trust them. First one to make a wrong move—use that scattergun."

"Don't fret yourself none," Letterman said, his narrowed eyes glowing with satisfaction. "We ain't going nowheres. Just seeing old Red take you apart piece by piece is going to be worth more'n a fistful of dollars to us."

Starbuck regarded Longhorn's foreman shrewdly. The words he'd spoken were no more than sound, mere bluster. The underlying meaning was altogether different, reflecting a growing, if grudging, admission that the law had strength. Arresting and disarming them in the Valley Queen had been the first shocking step toward instilling it in their minds; it was now up to him to increase that respect by giving their champion the licking of his life.

He grinned tautly, and turned to Bishop. The marshal had Letterman and the riders backed up against the jail, while he himself stood to one side, well out of reach, with the shotgun leveled. Arlie was learning.

Holstering his weapon, Shawn released the buckle, tossed the belt and gun to Bishop's feet, and retreated farther into the street. Red, mouth split happily, fingers spread, followed at a half crouch. The big man would be slow but powerful; he dare not let himself get trapped, permit Red to seize him in those huge hands.

A voice in the crowd said, "Reckon this ain't going to take long. Red ain't been a blacksmith all these years for nothing."

Blacksmith . . . Starbuck's jaw tightened. He should have realized that. The man's size alone, the great shoulders and powerful-looking arms, made it apparent.

74

But the knowledge changed nothing, only increased the already recognized need to be careful. Abruptly, he halted, then dropped into the cocked stance of a boxer.

A shout went up in the street.

"One of them there fancy dancers! This here is going to be good!"

"Get him, Red. . . . Learn him how a man does some real fighting."

Red's grin spread wider. He bobbed, took two lumbering steps forward, his hamlike fists raised. Shawn dipped to one side, stabbed the big man with stinging lefts to the eyes, crossed with a hard right that brought a quick smear of blood to Red's nose, and moved away.

The man cursed as the crowd yelled again. He tried to wheel hurriedly, but his movements were slow, awkward. Starbuck, shifting like a shadow in the lamplight that filled the street, came in fast from the side. His balled left fist jabbed the blacksmith's eyes again, and the right smashed solidly into his jaw.

Red halted flat-footed, arms hanging loosely from his massive shoulders. He shook himself like some huge beast and endeavored to fix his gaze on Starbuck, poised temptingly before him. Suddenly he yelled, lunged forward, fingers clawing.

Shawn faded back a few steps, and took a step to his left. As Red thundered in, he drove a stiff blow straight into the man's belly, again jabbing him savagely in the eyes and nose.

Red staggered, wind gushing from his open mouth. More blood showed on his slack features. The yelling of the crowd was now a steady racket, but the encouragement was all for Starbuck now. Sensing the kill, they urged him to move in, to cut the towering blacksmith down. In contrast, Jack Letterman and the Longhorn riders watched in glum silence.

Shawn began to circle, keeping just beyond Red's reach. He studied the man closely, striving to gauge his remaining strength and willingness. Red's eyes were now puffed and nearly shut. Blood was flowing continually from his nostrils, and his crushed lips were swollen out of shape. Spraddle-legged, he hung motionless, sucking to recover his wind.

"Ready to quit?" Starbuck asked, drifting in close.

Red swore, shook his head, and grabbed for Shawn's arm. Starbuck easily avoided the attempt, pivoting away. As the big man sought to follow, he spun, nailing him with a solid uppercut that started low and traveled the full distance.

The blacksmith rocked back on his heels, a dazed look in his eyes. Shawn grinned, admiration stirring through him. It had been a lucky blow, the kind a man seldom gets to swing except when fighting a slow-moving opponent. It would have felled any ordinary man in his tracks. Red had only staggered—but he was hurt. His jaw hung open, his blood-smeared face was slack, and his shoulders were limp.

"Enough?"

At Starbuck's question Red wagged his head numbly, and again moved forward. Shawn halted him with lefts to the mouth, and crossed with a crackling right, again to the chin. The blacksmith's knees wavered as the yells from the crowd increased. He took a half step to the side, tried to catch himself, failed, and went down full length into the dust.

Cheers filled the night as the crowd surged in. Ignoring the press, Shawn crossed quickly to Bishop's side, picked up his gun belt, and strapped it about his waist. Drawing the weapon, he nodded to the lawman and stepped to where Letterman and his men were waiting.

"You two," he said, pointing at the nearest in the line, "pick him up and get him inside."

The punchers moved hurriedly to comply. Starbuck, motioning the remaining men into the jail while Bishop covered them, followed the pair to where Red lay. Gun in hand, he stood to the side while they hoisted the blacksmith to his feet, hung his arms over their shoulders, and began to half drag, half carry him toward the door.

Voices were shouting congratulations at Shawn, and hands reached out to clap him on the back, but he was only partly aware of it. Just beyond the corner of the jail he could see Carla Bishop, her features pale and soft-edged in the yellow glow. There was a smile on her lips, one of relief he supposed, but there could also have been a measure of pride.

He swore softly. The fight was a hell of a thing for her to witness. It had been a scene likely to turn her more than ever against the country in which Arlie was hoping to build a new life. Abruptly she turned away, disappearing into the shadows.

Shawn shifted his attention back to the two Longhorn punchers. They had reached the doorway to the marshal's office and were pulling Red through. Beyond them he could see Letterman and the remaining riders already in one of the cells. Bishop, shotgun held across his chest, waited nearby.

Moving on, he entered the building, kicking the door closed with a heel to shut out the clamor in the street. The rigid caution he had been careful to observe during the fight had been dropped, and he stood now, motionless, staring at the floor.

Maybe he had taken a foolish chance, but he had gauged Red's abilities correctly—and he had won. Men like those in the street and those being locked in the cell were impressed by such a display, and that was what mattered; in their eyes the prestige of the law had risen considerably, and that was what he had hoped to accomplish.

Pulling off his hat, not even dislodged during the altercation with the blacksmith, Starbuck dropped it on the desk and sank into one of the chairs. There was another encouraging aspect to the situation; Arlie Bishop had been able to induct the Longhorn crew into a cell without his assistance.

14

STARBUCK LEANED BACK AGAINST THE WALL, watching Bishop as he came slowly through the connecting doorway that opened into the adjoining cell-block room. The lawman's features were sober as he closed the panel, and crossed to his desk and sat down.

"You did fine," Shawn said, and then when Arlie made no acknowledgment of his words, added, "Something wrong?"

"Letterman. says we can be expecting to hear from the rest of the Longhorn bunch soon's they come in off night herd and learn what's happened."

"Figured that."

"Not the worst of it. Told me Max Eagle will be here tomorrow."

Shawn frowned. "How does he know?"

"He's in Silver City. Letterman sent word to him, telling how I'd gunned down Ward. Says Max'll probably climb on his horse and come right back." "That's likely. How far is Silver City?"

"Short day's ride."

Starbuck considered that in silence and nodded. "Means the man Jack sent will get there by morning, and if Eagle leaves right off, he'll ride in sometime in the afternoon, tomorrow."

Bishop stirred, sighing deeply. "Well, expect there's no use worrying about it. If he kills me, he kills me. . . . Be bad for Carla and the baby."

"You gone back to giving up before he even gets here?"

"No point fooling myself. Idea you had for handling

79

Letterman and the others worked out fine. Actually had me feeling like I was an honest-to-God marshal there for a bit."

"You were—"

"With your help—and I'm thanking you for that, for taking it on yourself to work over Red, too, and call their bluff. But we both know that's about as far as you can go. Rest of it—standing up to Max Eagle—is something I'll have to do myself, and you know how that'll end up."

Arlie paused and rubbed his palms together thoughtfully. "Pity, too. Liked the feel of being a real marshal, of doing the job the way it's supposed to be done. Really think I understand what it's all about now—what this star I'm wearing represents."

"A little time to practice, and you'll be all right. Already got this town looking at you differently. Expect even Grissom's changed his mind some."

"I owe that to you, too."

"All I did was back you up. Credit for the way it turned out goes to the marshal—and that's you. That's how they'll see it, same as they won't forget it."

"Well, there's one thing folks around here sure won't be forgetting, and that's how you took on Red Weaver and cut him down to size. Never saw anything like that in my life. Why, he never touched you!"

"Wasn't about to let him grab me in those big paws of his," Starbuck said grimly. "He could break a man in two."

"I noticed before that belt buckle you're wearing. Didn't realize it meant you were a champion fighter of some kind. I figured it was something fancy you'd picked up to wear."

Starbuck looked down at the ornate silver oblong.

"Not mine actually. Belonged to my pa. He learned how to box from some Englishman, and got real good at it. Gave exhibition matches around Muskingum every chance he had."

"Then he was a champion?"

"No, but he could've been if he'd wanted, I suppose. He was more interested in farming, though. When he died, the buckle—a bunch of the neighbors got together once and presented it to him—came to me."

"Not all you got from him, I'd say," Bishop murmured, smiling. "Seems he passed along the know-how, too."

Shawn nodded, his thoughts flashing back to the time when he and Ben were growing up. No day passed that Hiram Starbuck did not spend at least one hour tutoring them in the art of boxing. On Saturdays the training sessions were usually much longer.

"Taught my brother and me both," he said. "Wanted us to always be able to protect ourselves, was the way he put it. A man's fists and his ability to handle himself were important back there. Nobody ever thought about carrying a gun unless he was going hunting."

Bishop bobbed his head. "That's the way of it where I came from. At home only a policeman ever wore a pistol, and a lot of them just carried a billyclub. Seeing every man you meet out here walking around with a revolver strapped to his middle surprised me—scared me a bit, too."

"Time'll come when you won't see that in the West, I expect. Most towns have a law against it now—just like the one you enforced here this evening. Folks haven't reached the point yet where they'll demand its enforcement in every town, but it'll be that way."

"I'd do it if I was to stay on the job," Arlie said.

81

"Now that the idea's been put across, I'd keep it going, enforce it all the way. Don't think it'd be too much of a problem, either. Pretty sure the townspeople would be for it, and outsiders riding in, seeing nobody else wearing a gun, probably wouldn't object to taking off theirs."

"Usually the way it works. Just have to make a start, and you've done that."

"I can get some new signs painted—big ones on real boards so's they'll last—and nail them up on all four sides of town where they won't be overlooked. Can have it put right on them that wearing a gun is illegal and that they're to be turned in to me at my office."

"Saloonkeepers can help you there. There are a lot of towns where a man has to hand over his weapon when he walks into a saloon."

"Could make it a choice—either check their guns with me or at a bar. Wouldn't matter as long as they shed them when they got into town. Place would seem a lot more civilized then, not seeing every man you met with a big pistol hanging on his hip."

"Guess it's the sign that a place is growing up," Shawn said. But it would be a time yet before it became a generally accepted idea, he knew. The settlements that enforced such a regulation were few, and the farther west a man rode the scarcer they became. Such a day would eventually arrive, however; civilization had a way of surmounting all obstacles.

"Might have to get myself a deputy," Bishop said. "Be a little hard for one man to look after everything, to see that no laws are broken. . . . And this jail ought to be fixed up, made to look like something. You be interested in a deputy job?"

Starbuck smiled, shaking his head. "No. Obliged to

you, but I'll be riding on in a few days."

"Oh, yeh, looking for your brother. Sure would like to have you."

"Be easy to find somebody around town."

"Expect so. Could use him as a sort of combination jailer and office man. He could watch over things while I was out, then when I needed help, he could step in and side me like you did."

"Be a good arrangement. The law would really mean something around here."

Arlie Bishop bobbed enthusiastically, his eyes alight as he envisioned the future. Then he abruptly settled back, a stricken look coming into his eyes. "Aw, what the hell am I prattling about," he said heavily. "Come sundown tomorrow I'll be a dead man. That's the only thing I can look forward to."

Starbuck waited out a long minute. "That mean you're aiming to stand up to Max Eagle?"

"No way out of it. Feel now like I can't let the law down—go crawling to him."

"Any plan?"

"The thing we used here tonight—ordinance against wearing a gun. Figured I could maybe talk him into turning his in, perhaps even get the drop on him and make him do it. Have a chance then to explain how Ward got killed."

"He won't give you time to do much of anything."

Bishop's shoulder lifted and fell. "Only way I can think to handle it—short of running."

"That's one answer, all right."

"Made up my mind I won't do that. Seems like I've been doing that all my life—running from hard times, bad luck, poverty. It stops here. Either I'll make it or I'm dead."

"What about your family?"

"Carla has some relatives in New York. She can take the baby and go live with them. Probably be better off, anyway. Jeannie can grow up in a decent place."

"But without a pa, and it'll be hard on Carla no matter what you think."

"Maybe so. It's the way it'll have to be, however. Got no choice."

Starbuck stirred, got to his feet. "Let tomorrow take care of itself—and there's no reason to lose any sleep over it. Go on home, I'll see you here in the morning."

Arlie rose, a grateful smile on his lips. "You sure you don't mind hanging around here looking after things?"

"Not a bit. Can catch a few winks on that bench if I feel the need." He drew back from the doorway, allowing the lawman to pass. "Don't think it's likely, but if some of the Longhorn bunch shows up looking for trouble, I'll fire a shot . . . Good night."

"Night," Bishop replied, and then added in a wistful voice, "man ought to spend his last night alive with his family. I'm thanking you for the favor."

15

SHAWN STOOD LISTENING to the thud of Bishop's boot heels moving across the landing, then the quieter, muffled thump as he stepped down into the dust and turned for home. The lawman had made his decision, one that could only have fatal consequences. He was hopelessly outclassed by Max Eagle, and the killer would show him no mercy—all of which he was aware. Arlie Bishop, all other shortcomings notwithstanding, was a brave man.

Disturbed, Starbuck stepped into the doorway and looked out into the night. Overhead the stars were a sprinkle of silver dust and nuggets on a blue-black canopy. The air was crisp, conveying the clean, good smell of wood smoke and the quavering notes of a woman inside the Valley Queen singing the melancholy ballad "Lorena" to the plinking of a piano. Elsewhere along the street windows were dark, the merchants having at last closed up shop and gone home, leaving Tannekaw to the saloons and Ruby McGrath.

It was a good town, he thought, one where a man could dig in, grow, make a mark for himself. It had problems, of course; what settlement did not? But time would pass and they would be overcome. He guessed he could understand why Arlie Bishop had determined to run no more; he at least had gained a small foothold here, however small—something he'd never managed to accomplish elsewhere.

A pity the cards were all stacked against him. Eventually he would have developed into a good lawman. He had acquired the feel for it, discovering within himself that strange, undeviating devotion for the law that only dedicated men experience. Given the chance to become proficient with a gun, he undoubtedly would not only be a credit to his profession but to the town he protected as well.

Starbuck stirred restlessly. Arlie would never have that opportunity, for, as he had said in that bitter, lost way, he would be dead by the next sundown. And there was nothing he could do about it, Shawn realized. He could not take Arlie's place, face the gunman for him; Max Eagle would accept satisfaction only from the man who had shot down his brother. It was an affair in which no substitutes were permitted.

The pathetic notes of the old war song ended in a burst of cheers. The pianist struck up a more lively tune, one overridden now and then by laughter and shouts. That the Valley Queen enjoyed the major portion of the town's business was evident; only two horses stood at the rack fronting the Red Mule, and none at all at the Silver Dollar.

Weary, troubled by his thoughts of Arlie Bishop and the inescapable fate that awaited him, of Carla and the uncertain future that she and her small daughter faced, he turned slowly, reentered the office, and sat down at the desk. Within him a conviction was growing, gaining strength, refusing to be ignored; he could not let Arlie Bishop die. He must find a way to keep him alive, while still satisfying Max Eagle.

He sat stone still in the dim light, considering the problem. Earlier he had toyed with the idea of aiding Bishop in some manner, but he had not gone into it deeply, contenting himself with letting it ride while matters took their course. Now he stood before the cold, brutal wall of decision; either he *find* a means or else forever after bear the stinging lash of his own conscience.

How—and assuming he could come up with a plan that would put him in Bishop's stead, what were the possibilities of his own survival when he faced Max Eagle?

He had never wasted much time considering his own capabilities with a six-gun. Whenever it had been necessary to use the weapon on his hip, he had found himself able to meet the situation. He supposed he was considered fast, probably better than average, and he knew that he was accurate—a necessity that chance acquaintance had impressed upon him when he first began the search for Ben.

"Might be a man can outdraw you," he'd said, demonstrating his own amazing skill, "but if pulling fast causes him to miss, then it ain't worth a damn to him. It's being fast and still putting the bullet where you want it that counts."

Shawn had listened well and taken the gunman's advice to heart, practicing diligently to perfect his draw and yet maintain accuracy. When they had finally gone their separate ways, Starbuck felt he could at least hold his own if ever the occasion arose where his life depended upon the forty-five riding on his hip—an assumption that proved correct in the months that followed.

But he was not fooling himself. For a man such as Max Eagle to gain the reputation he enjoyed, he would have to be good, and one who was also aware of the need for both speed and precision. The fact that he had never heard of the man meant little; only once before had he been through that particular part of New Mexico Territory, and there were those who preferred to stay within their own bailiwicks, where they could enjoy the advantages of local prestige.

Letterman . . . . He apparently was one of those who worshiped at the gunman's shrine. Perhaps he could learn a few facts pertaining to the man from him. Rising, Shawn moved to the connecting door, opened it, and stepped into the room. The prisoners were all in one cage. Some were slumped on the cot, others on the floor. In one corner he saw the blacksmith, Red; the man had drawn off to himself as much as the confines permitted. Both eyes were swollen shut, and his mouth and nose were puffed badly out of shape.

The Longhorn foreman rose and moved to the door of the cell, his features sly, expectant. "Letting us go?"

Starbuck shook his head. "Up to the marshal."

Letterman shrugged indifferently. "Makes no difference, I reckon. Sleeping here's the same as sleeping somewhere else. Max'll turn us loose tomorrow when he shows up—if some of the boys don't beat him to it."

"Don't bet on it," Shawn murmured. Then, "You set big store by this Max Eagle. Plain fact is I've never heard of him, and I've done quite a bit of traveling."

"You'll know him after tomorrow—and you sure won't be forgetting him. If you was half smart, you'd climb on your horse right now and be long gone before he shows, because he won't be figuring you for no friend, backing that tin star the way you been doing."

"Maybe so . . . He's great shakes with a six-gun, I take it."

"You take it right! He's killed sixteen men, not counting blacks and Indians and Mexes. Ain't no telling how many he's cut down if you was to tally all of them."

Starbuck leaned back against the wall, folded his arms across his chest, and wagged his head. "Sure is a puzzle why I never came across him. Seen plenty of the other top guns Allison, Tim Carnavan, Earp, Charlie Leslie, and such. None of them ever mentioned him, either."

"Expect they know him, just the same."

"I'm wondering. Seems to me somebody, somewhere, would have talked about him if he's big as you claim he is."

Letterman's features darkened. "You saying I'm lying to you'?"

"Nope, just can't figure why I never heard of a gunslinger named Max Eagle—until I got here."

"Well, he's the genuine article, all right. You'll find out tomorrow when he rides in from Silver City to take care of the greenhorn."

"Silver City where he lives?"

Jack Letterman shrugged. "Naw, got hisself a saloon and gambling joint up Colorado way. Come down to do some betting on the big fight that's coming off in Silver tomorrow—that's how it happened he was close. Ward was aiming to make the ride up there tonight, join with him. They ain't seen each other in a couple of years. Was going to do a little betting hisself."

A stillness had come over Shawn Starbuck. After a moment he said, "What kind of a fight?"

Longhorn's foreman spat into a corner of the cell. "Heard Ward say it was sort of a championship thing. Was to be between some big miner who'd licked everybody around there and one of them fancy boxers—like you."

16

STARBUCK DREW HIMSELF UP, senses tingling keenly. *A fancy boxer.* Ben—could it be Ben?

"Eagle mention any names—the fighters, I mean?"

Letterman reached into his shirt pocket for his sack of Bull Durham and its sheaf of thin, brown papers, and began to roll a cigarette. "Don't recollect what the miner was called. The fancy-dan's handle was Friend, seems."

Shawn started visibly, struck by the unexpectedness of it all. He had found Ben—assuming he was right in the belief that his brother had adopted the alias Damon Friend—and he was less than a short day's ride away. The search was over, finished, had come to an end at last. He had often wondered how he would feel at that moment of fulfillment. Curiously, he now found himself detached and disbelieving.

"You sure of that name?"

Letterman scratched a match into flame, touching it to the twisted tip of his smoke. "Hell, yes, I'm sure. Reckon I can hear."

A thread of suspicion began to worm its way into Starbuck's mind. Why would Letterman know the name of one man in the contest and not the other? He was aware that Shawn had come to the Slaughter Valley country looking for his brother; was the foreman making use of the knowledge to get him out of town for some reason?

Shawn thought back to that afternoon. Letterman had been in the Valley Queen with Ward Eagle when he'd made inquiries. But there had been no mention of Ben's boxing prowess nor of the name Damon Friend in their presence. Ruling out that possibility, he turned to a second; was Jack simply assuming that the boxer in Silver City was Ben, having concluded that two brothers would have had the same training in the art?

It wasn't likely. Letterman didn't strike him as being that smart—and whether he remained in Tannekaw for the arrival of Max Eagle was of small importance if what he'd said about the gunslinger was right.

"Why you so interested?"

Shawn roused himself from his deep thoughts. "Nothing much. Could be I know a man named Friend."

"Might be him, 'cause that was what Ward called him. Max had seen this jasper fight before and won some money on him. Ward was hoping to do the same."

It was Ben. It could be no one else. He was in Silver City putting on a match—probably to raise some cash—and then he'd move on just as he had done before. By riding out immediately he could get there around mid-morning, probably even before the fight was staged, and thus catch him before he rode on.

Starbuck felt a heaviness slip into him. He couldn't leave. He couldn't ride off, leave Bishop to face Max Eagle. Even though he had not made his intentions known to the lawman or anyone else, he couldn't do it. Bishop's blood would be on his hands, just as sure as if he'd shot him down himself, and that knowledge, lurking like a dark, accusing shadow in the back of his mind, was something he couldn't live with.

He stirred impatiently. If he'd minded his own business, stayed clear of trouble as he'd promised himself to do . . . but he hadn't. Now all he could do was hang around, see it through for Arlie Bishop—and for Carla's sake—and then hurry to Silver City in the hope that Ben would still be there . . . unless. . . . He

91

frowned, raising his glance to Jack Letterman.

"Any idea which road Eagle will be riding in on?"

The foreman smiled, glanced over his shoulder at the men behind him, and winked broadly. "Your feet starting to get cold, mister? You maybe thinking of pulling out and looking for the road Max won't be on?"

One of the punchers laughed, bobbing his head. "If it was me standing in your boots, danged if I wouldn't be doing the same. I sure wouldn't be anxious to meet him!"

"Be plenty smart," Letterman agreed.

"No doubt. Which road?" Shawn pressed.

If he knew for certain which route the gunman would be taking, he could head out, intercept him, settle things for Arlie Bishop, after which, assuming he was still able, he could hurry on to Silver City.

"How the hell would I know that? Could be he'll come across the mountain trail, or maybe he'll follow the main road—the one the stagecoach takes. And then there's another one the ranchers use, a sort of shortcut. All I can say is he'll pick the one he figures'll get him here the quickest."

Starbuck turned, made his way back to the lawman's office, and sank into the chair behind the desk. Trying to choose the road Max Eagle would take would be a gamble, one where the odds were three to one, and he couldn't afford to lose. If he failed to guess right, Arlie Bishop would die.

But what of his own needs? His life, from the day of his father's death, had been based upon finding Ben, clearing up pressing matters of the past so that he could have a future; was he to lose the first and only opportunity presented to him since it all began, and because of someone else?

Never before had he been this near to success; always it had been a rumor, a tip, that had led him on, unconfirmed, but information that seemingly indicated the person concerned was Ben. And each time he had arrived too late. Consequently, he was never certain that it had been his brother. But there was little doubt here.

The quest was ended—but it would have to start again. He had found Ben, yet he could not see him, talk to him, bring to a close the problems of the past. He could only hope that when, and if, he reached Silver City, it would not be too late, that Ben, for some reason, had stayed over. Judging from previous occasions, however, he had little faith in the possibility.

Starbuck's morose thoughts came to a halt as a step sounded on the landing. He glanced up, hand sliding unconsciously toward the pistol on his hip. It could be some of Longhorn's riders coming to break Jack Letterman and the others out of jail. A moment later his fingers fell away from the butt of the forty-five. It was Carla Bishop.

17

SHE HALTED JUST WITHIN THE DOORWAY, eyes dark and remote in the soft glow of the lamps. Her hair had been pulled into a bun at the back of her neck. Starbuck rose slowly.

"No place for you," he said, frowning.

Carla smiled, moved out of the entry, and sat down on one of the chairs against the wall. "Seems that's something I've never found," she murmured. "Perhaps I never shall."

The faint odor of her perfume touched Shawn. He looked away, and still frowning, resumed his seat behind the desk. They were thinking of two different things; he had meant her being alone with him, dressed as she was, in the late hours of the night. She was referring to her life in general.

"You will," he said. "Everyone does. It's only that it's taking longer for you—and Arlie."

She studied her clasped hands. "I wonder. We've drifted around from one place to another all our married lives, and we've never yet made a home."

"Maybe this is the time."

Carla raised her glance to him. "We both know better, don't we? By this time tomorrow, Arlie . . . it will all be over."

She did not break at the thought, nor did tears appear. She had simply made a statement of truth in a calm and direct way, as if she had become accustomed to facing such facts.

"Could be you're wrong. He's not the same man he was yesterday—or even this morning."

"Only because you're standing by him. You can't do that forever—not even tomorrow when that man comes to kill him."

"Maybe he won't get here. Something may happen, or it could be it's all talk. I've seen it work out that way before."

Carla Bishop shook her head wearily. "He'll come. That's how it's always been for us—something always turns up to destroy us, ruin our plans."

"Could be different this time," Starbuck said, quietly stubborn. "Arlie know you were coming here?"

"No, he's asleep. I was restless, decided to take a walk, get some fresh air. I saw you through the window and stopped by . . . Are you leaving tomorrow?"

"Figure to be around a few days longer."

"After that where will you go?"

"Tucson, if I don't find my brother here," he said, relieved at the change of subject. "Think he might be working for one of the ranchers in the valley."

He was lying to her, of course; he knew exactly where Ben was, but to reveal the truth would set her to wondering why he did not ride out immediately, and that would call for an explanation he could not give.

"Is it so important that you find him?"

"To us it is. Pa's estate can't be settled until I find him and take him back to Muskingum. It's written that way in the will."

"Did he run off from home?"

Shawn nodded. "When he was about sixteen. He and Pa had a big row over a chore Ben was supposed to take care of but forgot. Pa was always strict with us about things like that—not mean, but strict. The day ended up with Ben leaving, saying he'd never be back. Was the truth. We never heard from him again."

"Your mother, was she alive then?"

"Died about two years before. As long as she was around she sort of kept things peaceful between them. After she was gone it was different."

"I know," Carla said quietly. "I lost my parents when I was young, too. Both of them. Spent several years after that moving from one relative to another, trying to find a home. None of them ever really wanted me, so I never did find one. Then I met Arlie. Thought I was through looking, that at last I'd have a home of my own. Soon found out I was wrong."

She fell silent. The tinkling of the piano in the Valley Queen drifted softly through the night, and for a time she listened, eyes partly closed and far away.

"Oh, I wish tomorrow would never come!" she said abruptly, making a small, helpless gesture with her hands. "I—I wish there was some way I could make everything just stop!"

"Guess that wish has come to all of us at some time or another, and nobody yet's been able to figure out how to do it. About all we can do is take things as they come, make the best of it."

"I know, but I can't help wishing. . . Have you been looking for Ben ever since he ran off?"

"No, I stayed on the farm with Pa for a few years, until he died, then I began. Had no money. It's all tied up until I find him, so it's taken longer than it should. Every now and then I run out of cash and have to find myself a job and work for a spell."

"As a cowhand?"

"Anything I can find."

"Then I expect you've done about everything and been about everywhere."

He nodded. "Stagecoach driver, deputy sheriff,

marshal, trail hand—had a taste of it all from one end of the country to the other. Even did some pick and shovel mining down in Mexico once."

"And that special kind of fighting—boxing, I think it's called. Arlie told me about it he didn't know I was watching."

"Not something you or any woman ought to see."

Her small shoulders moved slightly. "I've seen men fight before, but not the way you did. Arlie said your father taught you."

"He was an expert. Called it the Queensberry style."

Carla's eyes were suddenly bright. "It was terrible—wonderful! That man was so huge, so strong, and yet he was utterly helpless!"

Starbuck looked away, not proud of the memory. "Hated cutting him up like I did. Didn't even know the man, but it was something that had to be done."

"Arlie said you could probably be a champion boxer if you wanted."

"Something I don't want. Use my fists only when I have to. What I want is what most every man wants—a home of my own, a wife, and family."

She faced him soberly. "You'll never have it if you spend your life looking for your brother. One day it will be too late."

"I've thought of that but the answer always comes out the same. There's nothing I can do about it until Ben's found and I settle things the way Pa wanted. Guess I could get along without my share of the money, but I can't be sure about Ben. He could be needing his part bad."

"He may be dead. Have you considered that?"

"Plenty of times."

"But you go on searching just the same—"

97

He nodded, standing fast in his determination to say nothing of Silver City and of Ben's presence there. If she was aware of that, she would relay the information to Arlie, and both would insist that he ride on, forget them and their problems—which he could not do.

"I—I hope you find him soon," she said then, rising. "I guess I'd better go. Talking to you has helped. I think I can sleep now."

"Good," Shawn said, also coming to his feet. "Do you want me to walk you home?"

"No need—it's not far. . . . Will there be other trouble tomorrow—besides that man, I mean. Arlie mentioned something about the friends of the cowboys you've got locked up. They might come, he said."

"No way of knowing for sure."

"But they could. They're used to having their way around here, doing what they please."

"That's all changed now. Knowing that probably is making them think twice about stirring up things. Most of the men working for Longhorn are just regular cowhands, and now that they've found out we won't put up with their foolishness, they'll settle down and act right. I think all the troublemakers are in the cell."

Carla turned to the door, hesitated. "I—I hope I'll get a chance to see you tomorrow. If not, I want to thank you now—"

"I'll be around . . . No thanks necessary, anyway."

"Yes, there is. We've had no friends here except you. I only wish you could have come sooner. Maybe things would've worked out some other way, and Arlie wouldn't be facing a tomorrow that could be his last."

"May not end that way. You need to hope a little."

"I grew tired of hoping a long time ago," she said in a falling voice. "And, as long as I'm wishing, I guess I can say I wish we had met sooner—you and I. I mean years ago, before it was too late. . . . Good night."

Shawn stood motionless behind the desk, eyes on the now-empty doorway where she had been, while her final words seeped into his mind. After a time he shrugged. He could wish that, too, but changing the past was an impossibility; too late was forever too late.

Moving out from behind the desk, conscious of the faint, lingering odor of her perfume, he closed the door and dropped the bar into its brackets. Then, drawing the window blind, he settled again into his chair. He'd best get a few winks of sleep; daylight would come only too soon.

18

STARBUCK WAS UP WITH THE SUN and already waiting for Arlie Bishop when he came in the next morning. The lawman appeared rested, but there was a gray grimness about him that could not be overlooked. He greeted Shawn with a slight nod.

"No trouble?"

"Nope."

"Get any sleep?"

"All I need."

Bishop stood his shotgun against the wall. "Want to say again I'm beholden to you—not only for taking over for me last night but for some of the things you said. Got to thinking about them before I dropped off. I'm telling you now I'm going to do the best I can today. If I come through it, fine; if not, well, that's the way it'll be."

Arlie had changed considerably, Shawn realized. He was more sure of himself, more in command. He would make a good lawman now, as well as provide that home Carla had so long hoped for, if he survived the hours that lay ahead. . . . And survive them he would, Starbuck vowed silently. That would be his contribution to their lives.

"Time we was getting a bite of breakfast," Bishop said briskly. "Carla wasn't awake when I left, and I didn't want to disturb her. Let's take a walk over to the Lone Star."

Picking up the double-barrel, he checked its loads, hung it over his forearm, and stepped out into the open. Shawn followed, pulling the outer door closed and

100

locking it.

It was still early, and only a few townspeople were up and about as they moved into the center of the street and pointed for the restaurant at its lower end. Starbuck stole a glance at the man beside him and felt a stir of satisfaction. Bishop carried himself rigidly erect, shoulders squared, hat set forward on his head. Sunlight flickered on the star pinned to his vest and upon the barrels of the weapon riding lightly on his arm.

He could see faces turned to them from inside store windows as they passed, and he wondered what thoughts lay behind those impassive stares. Did they still feel Arlie Bishop was wrong, that he was a loss insofar as the law was concerned? There would be some, he was certain, who had revised their opinion.

They reached the Lone Star, entered the building, and sat down at one of the tables. It was evident they were the first customers of the day, and almost immediately the owner bustled out from behind a partition that separated the kitchen from the dining area, wiping his hands on his apron as he came. His eyes fell upon the two men, briefly registered surprise, and then he smiled.

"Morning, gents. Breakfast?"

Shawn nodded. "Eggs, bacon, and coffee for me."

"Same," Arlie said. "And I'll be needing seven more orders of the same. Got prisoners to feed."

The café man rubbed his palms together. "Fine. I'll get them ready while you're eating so's you can take them when you leave."

"Send them over," Bishop said.

The man frowned. "Ain't got nobody handy right now I can use. Figured you could—"

"Got other things to think about besides toting grub for a bunch of cowhands, Joe," the lawman said curtly.

"How about some coffee now?"

The restaurant owner shrugged, retraced his steps to the kitchen, and returned shortly with two thick mugs and a small pot. Setting them on the table, and still clearly puzzled and disturbed by Bishop's attitude, he again retired to the area behind the partition and began to prepare the orders.

Shawn smiled faintly. Arlie Bishop had at last gotten the idea. He was making it known that he was the marshal, and demanding the respect that should be accorded the position. If he didn't falter he was well on the way to success.

Their food came. They ate in silence, rose, and paid their checks to the café owner who pocketed the coins in lieu of a cash box.

"Them other breakfasts—" he said hesitantly, "will be along soon's I can get somebody to carry them over."

"No big hurry," Bishop said. "Prisoners won't be going anywhere."

Again in the street Arlie halted on the restaurant's landing. "Expect I'd best take a walk to the other end of town—let them see I'm still on the job. . . . May be a surprise to some folks," he added with a tight grin.

"Be a good idea," Shawn agreed. "Want to make it alone?"

"I'd like to."

"Way it should be," Shawn said. "I'll be at the jail."

Bishop moved off immediately as if impatient to be on his way. Starbuck hung back until the lawman was well started and then, more slowly, returned to the office, taking up a stand in the doorway.

He could see people along the route pause, turn their attention to Bishop as he strode resolutely down the dusty strip separating the weathered buildings. As before, he was again erect, features set, sunlight dancing on the barrels of his shotgun. Arlie was giving Tannekaw something to look at—a taste of what it needed and could have.

Shawn turned, hearing a sound to his left. Joe, the café man, carrying a tray over which a white cloth had been draped, was moving up to him.

"Figured to tote these over myself before they got cold," the older man said, halting on the stoop. "Wasn't busy and couldn't be sure when somebody'd come along I could use to take them over. Ain't everybody can carry a tray without spilling something, anyway." He glanced toward Bishop, now at the corner of Billy Smith's Feed Store. "What's he up to?"

"Showing this town it's finally got itself a marshal," Starbuck replied, and stepped back to allow the man to enter.

Joe followed him through the office, waiting until the door leading into the cell block was open. Ignoring the sudden clamor of comments and questions from the men in the cage, he removed the cloth and, one by one, passed the plates of food and cups of coffee through the space provided in the grillwork for such purpose, and then returned to the adjoining room. His features were solemn.

"Maybe we've got us a marshal," he said glancing meaningfully at Shawn as he moved by. "But for how long?"

"Could be for longer than you expect," Starbuck said. Again closing the inside door, he trailed Joe back to the front entrance.

The café owner stopped on the landing, attention once more drawn to Bishop. The marshal had halted near the bakery, was in conversation with two men.

"Sure like to think so," he muttered. "I'm getting

plenty damn tired of having my place busted up by them hellions."

Shawn looked closely at the man. "Understood Grissom to say there was never any trouble—nothing serious, anyway."

"Henry was just talking, hoping to keep things from blowing sky-high and getting worse. We've all been hurt by that Longhorn bunch—and by some of the others, too. Not a man doing business in this town that hasn't had to dig down and shell out for fixing up his place after one of their hell-raisings.

"Something like that pinches a man right smart, but Henry was always for making no fuss about it. Said for us to just figure it part of the cost of doing business . . . Sure would like to think there'd be no more of them kind of costs," Joe added, and moved on.

That was good, Shawn realized. Undoubtedly there were other merchants who felt the same as Joe—possibly even Henry Grissom if he were to speak up honestly. Curious, he shifted his gaze to the general store. The mayor had come out onto the landing and was watching Arlie making his return. The lawman caught sight of the merchant at that moment. There was a slight break in his stride. Recovering quickly, he continued.

Grissom waited until he was directly in front of the store. Then, arms crossed, he stepped down into the dust.

"Bishop!" he called brusquely.

Anger swept through Starbuck. Grissom had made it a point to not address Arlie as the marshal, deliberately ignoring the courtesy.

"You turning them men loose?"

Bishop had halted, but he was not facing the mayor. His eyes reached beyond him, to Starbuck. He shook his head.

104

"Haven't given it any thought."

"Well, by God, you'd better!" Grissom shouted. "Rest of that Longhorn outfit'll be riding in here pretty quick, and they sure ain't going to take kindly to your jugging their friends."

"I'm not running things to suit them," Arlie said quietly. "I'm acting according to the law—your law."

"My law?"

"You were one of the men that drew it up. If you didn't intend for it to mean something, you shouldn't have written it."

Grissom appeared to be taken aback by the flat statement. He looked away momentarily, noting Starbuck standing in front of the jail, and the dozen or more townspeople halted on the sidewalks watching and listening. He stirred impatiently. "Then when are you aiming to turn them loose?"

"Law says they either pay a fine or serve time. I'll look it up and give them a choice."

"Should've done that last night. Keeping them in there like you've done just could make the rest of the Longhorn bunch take matters into their own hands."

"They're welcome to try," Bishop said, resuming his march. "I've got another cell waiting for them if they start trouble."

"You what!" Grissom exploded in an exasperated voice. "You think you can throw them—"

"Know I can," Arlie replied coolly, not slowing his stride.

Grissom opened his mouth to say more but checked himself as a look of satisfaction came over his features

"All right then, mister," he said in a smug sort of way, "maybe you'd better be getting ready. That's them coming now."

19

STARBUCK WHEELED. Six riders had turned into the lower end of the street, then halted. There was a brief consultation among them, after which half their number spun, and cutting back along Ruby McGrath's, disappeared. Shortly, the quick drumming of hooves sounded behind the buildings on the west as the punchers swept by, unseen.

Shawn's eyes narrowed. He pivoted slowly, placing his attention on the opposite end of the street. Almost at once the riders appeared, moving in near Gus Damson's stable and taking a stand, abreast, at the corner.

Starbuck's glance shifted back to Arlie Bishop. The lawman was aware of the change. The Longhorn crew had split, and they now faced him from opposite ends of the street. He gave the ones near Damson's a few moments studied consideration, then turned his head and contemplated the others.

"Well, Mister Marshal, time's come." Grissom's voice was taunting, tinged with triumph. "Bet you're wishing now you'd listened to me. The only thing you can do is get in there and turn them boys loose before their friends do it for you."

Bishop made no reply. In the tense hush that lay over the town Shawn eyed the lawman closely, searching for any sign of weakening If Arlie was having thoughts of backing down, they were not apparent.

"I'm telling you, Bishop, best you unlock that jail and let them go—right now!" Grissom's voice reached a high pitch. "I don't want them tearing up the place getting even with you!"

"They won't," Arlie replied, not taking his attention

off the men near Ruby McGrath's.

"What makes you think that? You suren' hell ain't going to stop them."

"Reckon I can try," Bishop said, and moved on, walking slowly down the center of the roadway.

He halted in front of the jail, nodding slightly to Shawn across the narrow distance separating them. The skin on his face had pulled tight, giving the planes an almost transparent look.

"Seems they've come," he said quietly. "Want to handle them myself."

"You're the dealer—your game," Starbuck replied.

More onlookers had come into the open, joining the already fair-sized audience observing the proceedings. Several were watching with excited interest while others plainly showed their worry over the possible outcome of the confrontation.

"You ain't catching them flat-footed like you did the others!" Grissom warned, "Better pay attention to what I said. Turn Letterman and them loose while you're still able!"

Bishop continued to study the riders near McGrath's. They were moving forward. Their counterparts at the upper end of town also swung into motion. Abruptly the two groups, riding three abreast across the width of the street, were closing in upon the lawman.

Shawn pulled away from the edge of the walk and took up a position more clearly in the open. He would honor Arlie Bishop's desire to personally handle the situation, but it was only prudent to let it be known that he was not alone.

"Telling you for the last time—you better let them boys go!" Grissom shouted, shaking his finger at Bishop.

107

Starbuck laid his hard, angry gaze on the merchant. "Why the hell don't you get inside, out of the way?" he snapped.

Grissom bristled. "Who you think you're talking to? I got more right to be out here than you!"

"Maybe so—and standing there like that you've got the same right to stop a stray bullet."

The mayor's head came up suddenly as if he had not realized the possibility He wiped at his mouth, wagging his head "Just what I'm trying to keep from happening," he said lamely "Don't want nobody getting hurt—"

"Stay out of it, Henry!" Clint Albers' voice called from the doorway of the hotel "Let the marshal be. He's trying to do something that should've been done a long time ago."

"Clint's right," a heavy-set man in front of the gun shop volunteered "Ain't called for, you butting in like you are."

Grissom flung a hot look at him, whirled, mounted the steps to the landing that fronted his store, and paused. "All right!" he shouted "Want you all to hear this—I ain't responsible for what's going to happen Don't forget that!"

"We'll remember," the husky man said, "whether it's good or bad."

The two groups of Longhorn riders had halted, a hundred yards or so still separating them. Bishop, a taut shape in the streaming sunlight, was about midway between. Abruptly the punchers swept off their hats, yelled, and dug spurs into the flanks of their mounts. The horses plunged forward, breaking into a hard gallop directly at the lawman, while the canyon between the buildings echoed with shouts

Alarm rocked through Shawn as he watched the

108

riders bearing down upon Bishop. Drawing his pistol, he stepped farther into the street. The lawman had not stirred, and then when the horses seemed almost upon him, he calmly raised his shotgun, threw a charge of buckshot into the ground a wagonlength ahead of the oncharging men coming at him from the lower end of the street, and quartered quickly to face the trio sweeping in on him from the opposite side.

The startled horses veered wide in the deafening blast of sound and rising dust and smoke. One of the riders, caught off balance, catapulted from the saddle and sprawled to the ground, while the two with him fought to control their mounts.

Starbuck grinned, his glance now on the men who had raced in from the direction of Damson's. The roar of the shotgun had cooled their enthusiasm quickly, causing them to swing off to the side and pull to a halt. "Just sit easy," Shawn drawled, hand resting on the butt of his pistol. "We'll see what the marshal's got in mind."

Bishop, cool and deliberate, broke the shotgun, dropped the spent shell casing at his feet, and slipped a fresh load into the barrel. The smoke and yellowish dust were now drifting lazily away, and the man spilled from his saddle had regained his feet; his companions had finally brought their mounts under control and were staring numbly at the lawman.

Without changing his stance, Bishop raised his left hand and made a beckoning motion at the riders halted near Starbuck.

"Get over here," he commanded in a hard voice.

The punchers crossed at once, meekly taking a place with the others. Shawn, keeping behind Bishop, stepped in nearer.

"You're all wearing guns," Arlie continued in the same tone. "Law against that. Shuck them—now!"

Only a dark-faced man with a scar across his chin failed to reach for his belt buckle and allow his holstered weapon to fall. Bishop considered him coldly.

"You're the one called Turley. That right?"

The puncher nodded, scowling. "If you figure to pull my iron, you'd best do some more figuring."

"I'm taking it, all right—one way or another," the lawman said, and raising his shotgun, leveled it at the man's head.

Turley swallowed, glancing sideways at his friends. "Ain't nobody ever pulled my iron," he mumbled.

"I am," Arlie said, his words clearly audible in the tense hush that filled the street. "Want you to get this straight. You're welcome here as long as you. don't come armed. Wear a gun and you're in for trouble."

The scar-faced man continued to scowl. Bishop settled the shotgun's stock firmly against his shoulder.

"Last chance."

"What about Jack—the rest of the boys?" Turley blurted in a desperate sort of voice.

"Locked up for the same reason. They couldn't see it my way."

The scarred man brushed at the sweat collected on his forehead. "You mean this here's a law we got to follow every time we come to town?"

"Right. No guns. Turn them in to me when you ride in. Nobody's excepted."

Turley relaxed. A sly grin cracked his thick lips. "That so? How about Max Eagle?"

Starbuck saw a slight break in the hard line Arlie Bishop's shoulders formed. He was aware of a hesitation.

"Goes for him, too," the lawman said, finally.

Turley's grin broadened. "Well, now, that's something I aim to be around to see," he said, loosening his belt and allowing his weapon to fall. "Yes, sir, it'll be worth shedding my iron for—watching you do that little thing—or trying to. You jugging us?"

Bishop shook his head. "Go on about your business— but keep out of trouble. I won't put up with any more of your wild doings. When you're ready to ride out, you'll get your pistols."

Shawn waited until the punchers had moved off, pointing apparently for the Silver Dollar at the upper end of town, and then stepped forward to assist the lawman in collecting the discarded gun belts. He could hear a low mutter of favorable comment along the street, although no one hurried forward to express himself.

It was there, nevertheless, Starbuck knew as he followed Arlie into the office, and the belief stirred a ray of hope into life within him. Maybe he wouldn't have to hang around after all. Bishop had been tested and had come through; now, with most of the town undeniably behind him and perhaps willing to help, he might be able to come up with a way for handling Max Eagle when he arrived. If so, there was still time to reach Silver City and talk to Ben.

Dumping the weapons into a back corner of the room, he turned to Bishop. The bubble of possibility inside him began to fade. Arlie had sunk into his chair. His face was chalk white and fear filled his eyes. His hands, clenched so tightly the knuckles stood out like bald knobs, were trembling violently. He lifted his gaze to Shawn.

"I was all right—fine," he murmured in a sick, exhausted voice, "just fine until Turley mentioned Max Eagle. Then all the sand seemed to run out of me."

111

20

ARLIE BISHOP WAS ON THE VERGE OF COLLAPSE. Shawn considered the shaken lawman in stony silence as the hope within him died. He could forget Silver City—and Ben.

"I'm admitting it," Bishop said, wiping away the sweat on his face with a forearm. "I'm plain scared—scared as hell everytime I think about Eagle showing up. He'll kill me sure."

"You're dead even before he gets here, feeling that way about it," Starbuck said wearily, settling onto a bench.

"How else can I feel? I know what I can do, and what I can't."

"The show you put on out there in the street wasn't done by a scared man. Took a lot of guts."

"That was different. They weren't Max Eagle—just a bunch of cowhands spoiling for trouble. When I got the jump on them they backed down. Eagle won't."

"Don't expect he will," Shawn admitted, "but you're climbing hills again before you get to them. This man may not be all he's cracked up to. Could be all talk, a lot of blow and nothing else."

Bishop stirred disconsolately. "He's a killer. No doubt of that and I won't have a chance against—"

"Still climbing those hills—"

"No, just being honest with myself."

"Have you changed your thinking from earlier this morning? Said then you'd go up against him, regardless."

"I know that—and I was still feeling that way until that goddamn Turley opened his mouth. Was different

112

up to then. I'd found out a few things about myself—mostly that I could be a man, could hold down this job, and do it the way it's supposed to be done, in spite of the loud talkers like Grissom. Then along came Turley, and I realized I was nothing when it came to somebody like Max Eagle—and knowing that sort of wiped out all the rest. You ever have that feeling?"

"Boils down to fear. Sure—and any man who tells you he's never been scared is a liar."

"Got a big notion inside me to run, to get the hell out of here before it's too late. But there's something else inside me that's holding me back, won't let me. It's sort of like being in a trap."

"That's just what it is, and the part that won't stand for you running is the real man in you."

"Real man!" Bishop echoed scornfully. "What good's a real man if he's dead? I'd be better off a live coward. At least I'd be able to look after Carla and Jeannie."

Shawn nodded. "That's one way to look at it."

Arlie was ignoring the fact that living with the memory of his own cowardice, knowing also that Carla was aware he had turned tail, would be a burden he'd find hard to carry the remainder of his life. But Starbuck made no mention of it. Bishop was suffering enough.

"There's one answer," Shawn said, uncertain now what the lawman's reaction would be to his suggestion. Earlier he had known; Bishop had declared his intention of facing Eagle, regardless of the probable outcome, but in the last few minutes he had changed.

"What's that?"

"Leave Max Eagle to me."

The lawman was utterly still for a long minute, and then allowing his shoulders to sag, he shook his head. "Obliged to you. That's one answer, sure enough—but ,

113

not the one for me. Think I've got the town swinging to me now, and dodging that killer would spoil it all. They're looking to me to stop him somehow."

"You've done more than they figured you could. I expect they'd help if you'd ask."

"Maybe, but if I did that then I'd be right back where I started. Can't you see that?"

"Not sure I do. Can't see how getting yourself killed is going to help much."

Bishop sighed, again wiping sweat from his face. "Just this—I'll either come out on top, by some fluke maybe, or I'll be dead, and then it won't make any difference to me. I'll be finished with it—everything."

Starbuck's eyes tightened. "Guess I see what you're driving at. If you live through it, fine. If you're dead it won't matter, because you won't be around to know it."

"Reckon that's what it amounts to. Everything's solved either way it goes."

"Except for your wife and daughter. Opens up a whole new batch of problems for them if you're gone."

"That's all I've ever given them anyway."

The lawman's voice broke. He, too, was right back where he started, Shawn realized, faced with the need to help a man afraid of what lay ahead for him, yet determined to meet it regardless of the outcome, while his own purpose in life went begging. If he could only persuade Arlie—

Starbuck's thoughts shifted. Outside in the street there was the sound of boots, of men speaking. Shawn rose, stepping to the doorway. A half a dozen or more townsmen were approaching. He recognized Clint Albers, the heavy-set individual who had stood in front of the gun shop, another he thought was Billy Smith. The rest were not familiar.

114

"You've got a delegation," he said, turning to Bishop.

The lawman hastily got to his feet, once again nervously brushed the sweat from his features, but he could not erase the brightness that filled his eyes. Silent, he waited as the men trooped into the small office and gathered in a knot before the desk. There were a few moments of confused shuffling about, and then hotel-owner Albers pushed a half step forward.

"Want you to know, Marshal, that we don't hold with Grissom in what he's saying."

Bishop nodded, then looked down. "Appreciate that."

"Henry's all right, and he's the mayor, but we figure he's wrong. We think it's high time a stop was put to all the tomfoolishness them cowhands have been getting by with—not just let it pass like he thinks we ought."

"He maybe can afford to do that," a man standing to Albers' left said. "He does plenty of business with Longhorn and the other outfits, but me—all I got's a little two-bit bakery, and everytime they bust my windows or tear down my hitchrack I got to dig deep for the money to do the repairing."

"Same here," another added. "Last time they got to cutting up, somebody threw a torch on my roof. Near burnt me out. Me and my family are still eating beans and sow-belly on account of that."

"We ain't the only people feeling this way," Albers continued. "There are plenty more around town who'd like to line up with you, only they don't dare. They're backing you just the same, however."

Arlie Bishop nodded. "Aim to give you the kind of law you want if—"

"Ain't no *if* to it," Albers cut in. "Seeing you take the wind out of Ike Turley and them others there a bit ago has proved you're our man. Can't be no doubt in

115

anybody's mind that you mean business."

"For a fact," the man behind him said, bobbing his head vigorously. "And keeping Letterman and his crowd locked up in spite of everything—that's something, too! Sure glad you finally decided to crack down. Reckon all the time before this you was just hanging back, getting the lay of things."

"Could put it that way, I guess," Arlie murmured.

"Well, it's a mighty welcome change, and a long time coming. Point we're here to make is that you go right ahead with however you want to run things. Grissom's the mayor, but he can't fire you unless the rest of the council agrees—which it won't. The majority's right here, and we're all of the same mind. You've got a free hand."

"Yes, sir, you plain do what you think's needed. We'll keep out of your way."

Slouched against the wall, Starbuck smiled cynically. *You've got a free hand to do what you want—even die for us if necessary,* was what they were telling Arlie Bishop. It was not a new and unusual situation. In fact, it was ordinary. Townspeople customarily were willing to stand by their marshal as long as it was his blood that might be shed. When a man pinned on a star he expected it to be that way.

"Now, we don't know what you're figuring to do about this brother of Ward's when he shows up," Albers said, "but seeing how you do things, we suppose you've got it all set. Anyway, we'll leave it up to you." The hotel man smiled, extending his hand. "Just want to say thanks—and good luck."

Bishop took Albers' fingers into his own, face taut and expressionless, nodding automatically to the remaining members of the deputation as they followed

116

the hotel man's example and filed out. When the last one had gone, he sank into his chair and looked up at Starbuck.

"You see now why I ain't got a choice? They're depending on me—me, worthless, useless old Arlie Bishop, who's never done nothing that amounted to a hoot in his whole damned life!"

"You had the chance to tell them about Max Eagle, admit you—"

"I'm not about to let them know I'm scared. For once I'm somebody, and I wasn't about to tell them that. I'd be right back crawling on my belly. No, by God, I'd rather get myself shot down than be nothing again! That make sense?"

Starbuck shrugged. "Sure. It's a little thing in a man that can grow plenty big. Folks call it pride."

Bishop was still for a long minute. Finally he sighed, wagging his head. "Whatever it is, I'm enjoying the feel of it—and what's more, I'd rather die proud, if that's what it is, than go back to being what I was."

21

SHAWN MADE NO REPLY TO BISHOP. Arlie wouldn't be the first, or the last, man to die because of his pride—and he'd find himself in some select company, many of whom were far better men than he could ever hope to be.

But it would be a senseless waste. While there were moments during the brief time he had known the man when there were doubts as to whether he could ever fulfill the role of a lawman, he was forced to admit that Arlie did possess those two most important requirements—the will and the desire. His one shortcoming was his fear of Max Eagle, which was understandable since he was being thrown against a famed killer before he had a chance to even familiarize himself with a gun, much less become adept.

That, however, was a problem that possibly could be dealt with; the question was, would Arlie Bishop continue to quail and break down in the future when threatened by the presence of some other touted gunman such as Eagle? If so, there was little point in laying his own life on the line for the man. It would be best halted here and now, forcing Bishop to swallow his newly discovered pride and seek some other means of livelihood.

It was a gamble, pure and simple, Shawn admitted, but the odds now favored Arlie. He was a far better, more confident man than he had been twelve or so hours earlier; indeed, his actions in the street, when he had stood his ground and taken Turley and his Longhorn toughs in hand, was a demonstration of cool thinking

118

and steady nerves—something to be expected only of a far more experienced man.

And Carla. She, too, was a factor in the problem, and could not be ignored. While making no spoken appeal to him, he had seen it in her eyes, had sensed it in her manner and the tone of her voice—a lonely, soundless cry begging him to help, to make it all work out for Arlie, for her, and for their young daughter.

It was not in Shawn Starbuck to turn away. He would have to see Bishop through his crisis and simply trust in the future, he realized. Earlier he had not been sure; his feelings had see-sawed back and forth, influenced by thought and circumstance; but now he knew for certain what he must do.

The sound of horses pulling up to the rack reached into the office. Starbuck swung about at once to the doorway, and Bishop came to his feet, mouth going taut, eyes widening. Shawn waved him back. It was not Max Eagle, only two punchers. Filling the entrance with his tall shape, he nodded to the men.

"Something I can do for you?"

"That sign saying we ain't to carry guns," the man nearest said, "we leave them here?"

Starbuck nodded, stepped out into the warm sunlight, and accepted their heavy belts. "Pick them up when you ride out."

"Yes sir. We're aiming to hang around, see all the fireworks. That's all right with you, ain't it?"

"Fireworks?"

"We was told Max Eagle was coming in for a showdown with the marshal. Was told right, wasn't we?"

Again Shawn moved his head. "Just keep off the street."

119

"Sure . . . You the marshal?"

"Deputy," Starbuck said, and turned back into the jail.

Bishop had resettled in his chair, attention seemingly drawn to the adjoining room, where one of the prisoners was rattling a tin cup against the bars. He glanced at Shawn as he entered. "More of the Longhorn bunch?"

"Don't think so. Asked if I was the marshal."

"Outsiders. Word must've got around."

"You can bet on it," Starbuck said, adding the belts to the others piled in the corner. "Can expect plenty of them, along with every cowhand in Slaughter Valley that can get off the job to show up here today."

"And all hoping to see me get my head shot off," Arlie said wryly.

"Not so much that as being plain curious. There's a lot riding on the outcome. If Eagle kills you, things won't be any different around here. If you down him, they know the honeymoon's over, and they'll have to look for some other town to do their hell-raising in."

Bishop grunted. "Reckon they've got no cause to worry."

"Nothing's for sure. Main thing is don't let them know that. You gave everybody a look at how a good lawman works, out there in the street this morning. You need to keep it up. If I were you I'd take a walk, do some looking around town, see if there's anybody who forgot to leave his gun off."

"But what about Eagle?"

"Forget him. Not much chance of him getting here until the middle of the afternoon, or even later. Gives you time to convince everybody you're the marshal and that you intend to give this town law and order if you have to jam it down their throats."

Arlie hesitated for a long breath and then moved out

120

from behind the desk. Picking up his shotgun, he checked its loads, squared his hat, and, without a word, stepped through the doorway into the street.

Shawn watched him cross to the center of the quiet, dusty strip, glance in both directions, and start toward the upper end, taking firm, slow strides, the shotgun hung over a forearm as he swung his glance from side to side. He was the exact picture of a lawman on the prowl, a shepherd of order and decency tending his flock, guarding it against the wolves who would pull it down and claim it for their own. Starbuck turned away. He hoped he could help Arlie Bishop live up to expectations.

Restless, seeking a means for passing the time, his eyes fell upon the pile of surrendered gun belts laying in the corner. There would be more to come. He'd as well make preparations for them.

Crossing to the desk he searched the drawers until he found a can of nails and a hammer. Selecting one of the bare walls, he drove two dozen or so of the spikes into the dry wood in rows at proper intervals. That accomplished, he hung the belts, with their holstered weapons, from the steel pegs, thus making them more convenient to handle.

Finished with that chore, he dropped back to the doorway, throwing his glance up the street. Bishop was standing in front of the bakery again, talking with three men. Shawn recognized them as part of the delegation calling upon Arlie to express their approval of him.

There was no one else along the walks, and any stranger putting in an appearance would think the town was taking a holiday. A hard grin pulled down the corners of his mouth. It amounted to about the same thing, he reckoned, paralleling the times in ancient

Rome that he'd read about in history books, when men were put into an arena and fought to the death, while a fascinated, bloodthirsty audience looked on in holiday spirit.

"Mister—"

Shawn wheeled at the unexpected voice. A young boy stood on the landing, his eyes reflecting the excitement that gripped him.

"Yeh?"

"Pa sent me—from the restaurant. I'm to get the dirty dishes from them breakfasts and ask if you'll be wanting seven dinners."

"Tell him to make it eight," Starbuck said, and led the boy into the adjoining room.

Ignoring the sullen looks and muttered questions of the prisoners, he stood to one side while the youngster piled onto a tray the dishes pushed to him through the opening in the bars.

"When the hell are we getting out of here?" Letterman demanded as the boy, carrying his load, turned back into the office.

"Up to the marshal."

"Ain't right, him keeping us locked up without no reason." There was a plaintive note in the foreman's voice.

"You know why you're in there."

"Packing a gun? That was something he just trumped up on us . . . What was that shooting a while back?"

"Rest of your friends. Marshal changed their thinking about the law, too," Starbuck said and closed the door.

He looked again into the hushed, deserted street. Bishop was on the return lap, walking the center line, erect, grim, and purposeful. Shawn waited until he had passed by, and then crossed to the chair behind the desk.

The minutes were dragging tediously. He almost wished Max Eagle would arrive and they could get it over with; the town could then breathe once more.

Time continued to crawl. Bishop reappeared, halted just outside the doorway, critically scanned the street, and entered. Sweat lay on his skin, and standing the shotgun against the wall, he removed his hat and mopped his face and neck as he sat down on the edge of the desk.

"Was some other punchers come in from the valley," he said. "They'd handed their guns over to the bartender at the Red Mule. I told them that was all right."

"Just so they took them off."

"Saw some kid come in here—"

"Was the boy from the restaurant after the dishes. I ordered dinner for the prisoners and one for myself. Figured you'd be eating with your family."

"Obliged," Arlie murmured. The strain he was under showed plainly in his eyes, in the tight lines around his mouth.

"What about them?" he said, jerking his thumb toward the cell block. "Reckon they ought to be turned loose?"

"Not until later. Better off in there, where they won't get in the way. Besides, what you told Grissom still holds. They've got time to serve or a fine to pay. Can't just let them go."

"Why not?" Bishop asked wearily. "What difference is it going to make now?"

"Plenty. You arrested them for breaking one of the town ordinances. There's a penalty for that. If you don't collect it then you're sidetracking the law and it won't mean anything."

Arlie mulled that over in silence. "Yeh, guess you're

right," he said. "I'll look up what the fine is for carrying a gun—or the sentence."

"Later," Starbuck reminded.

Bishop nodded. "Yeh, later," he repeated, and drew himself upright. "Guess it's about time to get myself a bite."

"Near noon ... You go ahead, I'll do my eating here."

"It make any difference how long I take?"

"Couple hours, no more than that," Shawn replied. "And when you get back figure on staying here, inside. Max Eagle ought to be showing up about then."

* 22 *

Two o'clock.

Arlie Bishop paced nervously back and forth in the restricting confines of his office. Starbuck, slouched in a chair cocked on two legs against the wall so he could look out through the doorway onto Tannekaw's sunlight-flooded street, studied the lawman closely.

Arlie's state of mind was much worse since the noon-hour visit with his wife and daughter, and his agitation was becoming increasingly more intense as the heavily charged minutes crept by.

"Expect you could use a drink."

Bishop paused. "Need more'n that," he snapped. "Whiskey won't help what's chewing at me."

"Worrying over it won't either. You're just tearing yourself up . . . Things will come out all right."

"Easy for you to say," the lawman shot back, brushing at his eyes. "You ain't the one that's dying."

Starbuck shrugged. "Dying's a fact of life. We all have to face it when our time comes—and that's something nobody knows for sure."

"I know—"

"You're just telling yourself you do. Could be something will happen and your card won't get turned up."

Bishop leaned over the desk, bracing himself with palms flat on its top, elbows stiff.

"You trying to tell me something—like maybe you're aiming to take my place?"

"Never said that."

"Well, if you are—forget it! I won't have you or

125

anybody else standing up to Eagle for me. If I can't handle him, then I can't handle this job, and that's something I've got to find out once and for all!"

"You can handle the job. You proved that. And given a little time, you can take care of the Max Eagles around here, too."

"That's not the question! This is now—and he ain't about to hold off, to wait until I've learned how to use a six-gun."

Shawn had no answer to that. Talking to Bishop, attempting to persuade him that it was only wise to accept help, was useless. He was a man caught between the promise of certain death and the determination to prove himself or die trying; in such a frenetic condition there was no reasoning with him. It was best simply to remain silent and pursue his own plans, as yet unformed, depending on the situation when it presented itself.

More cowboys rode in, some coming directly to the marshal's office and turning in their weapons, others going first to one of the saloons, apparently to verify the new and unexpected regulation before relinquishing their gear.

Time wore on. Shortly after three o'clock the Reverend Bright of the Methodist Church made his appearance. A tall, darkly clothed man with long, sallow features, he shook hands gravely with Starbuck and Arlie and then asked the lawman the usual question. "Is there anything I can do for you?"

Bishop smiled crookedly. "Not being dead yet, I'll say no. Later on you can do some preaching over my grave."

The minister nodded solemnly. "Not exactly what I meant, but a man facing—"

"Death?" the lawman supplied bluntly.

126

"Well, yes . . . I thought you might have some things not yet tended to. I'm offering you—"

"Forget about me," Bishop said, his manner softening. "Expect my wife could use some company. I'd appreciate your looking in on her."

"Of course," Bright murmured. "I'll go there now if you're sure there's nothing I can do for you."

"Nothing," Arlie said, and again took the hand offered him.

Bright turned away, walking in long, cranelike strides and reentered the street. Bishop watched him depart, then shrugged. "The undertaker will be showing up next, I reckon, measuring me for size and wanting to know what kind of a coffin I'd like."

Abruptly, he sank into his chair, and crossing his arms on the desk, bowed his head upon them. Shawn regarded the lawman sympathetically, wishing there was some way he could reassure him without tipping his hand, but it was not possible.

Bishop raised his head. "I was just thinking about what the parson said—what ought to be done. Got one favor I'd like to ask of you."

"Name it."

"If things go the wrong way, I'd like for you to see that Carla and Jeannie get headed back to New York. The town will owe me about a full month's salary. That, along with what she can get for selling the cow and the chickens and the stuff in the house that she won't need, ought to be enough to get them there."

"Probably won't be necessary."

"I'm asking you just the same."

"Good as done," Starbuck said, shifting his attention back to the street.

Two more riders came in to see the sights. It was a

127

wonder that some enterprising individual hadn't erected bleachers and sold tickets. He glanced again at the lawman. Arlie was once more slumped forward, head resting on his folded arms.

Four o'clock.

The dusty roadway between the twin rows of buildings was a vacuum filled only with tension. There were people inside the stores and nearby homes, but they were keeping well back from the windows, as if wanting neither to see nor become a part of the impending drama. It was as if all Tannekaw—the universe itself, in fact—had lapsed into a state of suspension and could not stir until the moment of adversity had passed.

Starbuck allowed his chair to rock forward and come to rest on all of its legs. Bishop looked up quickly at the sound.

"What's the matter?"

It was against Shawn's better judgment, but he felt the question should be asked. "You want to walk over, see your wife for a few minutes?"

Arlie shook his head. "No. Took care of that at noon. Going there now would only make it worse for both of us."

Starbuck got to his feet, stepped through the doorway onto the landing, and glanced about. There were at least a dozen horses at the Silver Dollar's hitchrack, and as many at the Red Mule. None stood in front of the nearby Valley Queen, and he guessed that the men who undoubtedly were inside had posted their mounts at the rear of the structure. The saloon's proximity to the marshal's office, where the confrontation was anticipated, dictated the more prudent location for their horses.

He swung his attention to the upper end of town. Max

128

Eagle would be entering from that direction. Silver City lay to the north. He thought of Ben, wondering if he was still there. The exhibition would be over by now, and had he been able to leave when he first heard of the proposed boxing match, he would now be there with Ben, talking over the past, making plans for the future. As it was, he could only hope that his brother, for some reason, would elect to stay over another day. If so, he could make the ride in time.

Pivoting, he stepped back into the hushed office. Arlie had not moved, still hunched over the desk. Shawn resumed his chair, again tipping it against the wall. The dragging, endless minutes were the worst part of all for the lawman, he knew. Each would seem an eternity, and each would be filled with the memory of what had gone before in the past and the thoughts of what the future could have held.

He would be a man steadily turning inward under the relentless ticking of the clock, while bitterness chilled his soul, changing his blood to ice; he would be a man savagely torn, suffering hell's own torments, reluctant to live, equally reluctant to die—fully aware that the one solution to it all lay beyond him.

And it was an impossibility for Arlie Bishop. By the nod of circumstance, he was incapable of measuring up to the test and overcoming Max Eagle. He would win out and live and have his acclaim, however, but at the cost of the personal victory over himself that he sought.

It was no muffled hoofbeat nor any warning cry of a friendly voice along the eerily forsaken roadway that brought Starbuck to his feet silently, only some fathomless inner instinct. Grim, he eased quietly onto the landing, looked to the north.

A solitary rider was entering the street.

* 23*

STARBUCK STUDIED THE HUNCHED FIGURE IMPASSIVELY. A squat man easing forward on his saddle, both hands resting on the horn, as if wearied by a long, tiresome ride . . . *Max Eagle,* he thought, but he must be sure. There was no room for error.

The hush deepened along the street, and tension became almost tangible as the rider advanced steadily. He drew abreast Miss Purdy's dress shop, raised his head slightly, searched the bleached facades stolidly, as if seeking one particular place. Starbuck's jaw tightened. It was Max Eagle. There could be no mistake—the same husky build, the same dark features and cold, ruthless eyes.

Wheeling, Shawn retreated softly into the office. Bishop had not stirred. Starbuck moved around until he stood beside the lawman, waiting until he heard the muted thud of the gunman's horse in front of the jail and the silence following, when he had halted at the hitchrack. He looked down at Bishop. "Arlie," he said.

The lawman lifted a ravaged face to him. Starbuck's knotted fist swung hard, connected with the point of the man's chin. Bishop's head snapped back, eyes rolling to the top of their sockets. A groan slipped from his sagging mouth as he slumped deeper into his chair.

"Marshal!"

Starbuck ignored the harsh summons from the street. Reaching down, he unfastened the star on Arlie's vest, pinning it to his own shirt pocket. He started across the office, left hand instinctively dropping to the pistol on his hip, assuring himself of its presence, of its freeness in the holster.

He hesitated, glancing at the shotgun Bishop had propped against the wall. In the minds of the townspeople of Slaughter Valley, Arlie and the double-barreled weapon were associated. He would have to use it despite his preference for a forty-five. Picking it up he broke it and checked the loads. It was ready. Grasping it in his left hand, one finger on the forward trigger, he stepped up to the doorway.

Except for Max Eagle, there was no one to be seen. That was as he'd hoped it would be. Keeping within the entrance, he faced the gunman.

Eagle, broad features expressionless, regarded him with lifeless eyes.

"You the marshal?"

"I'm wearing the star," Starbuck replied coolly. Behind him he could hear Bishop stirring about as consciousness began to return.

"I'm Max Eagle. Got a score to settle with you."

"Best you forget it—move on."

"It was my brother you gunned down. I don't let something like that pass."

"Up to you. Make any difference if I tell you he asked for it?"

"None," Eagle said, abruptly uncoiling like a suddenly released spring. His left hand flung wide, the right swept down, returning in a glinting arc.

Starbuck rocked to one side. The shotgun, held as if it were a pistol, tipped up, bucked in his tight grasp as he triggered the charge of buckshot. Max Eagle lifted off the ground as the load slammed into him and hurled him backward a full stride. The gun in his clutching fingers rapped sharply as he went sprawling into the dust, its bullet harmlessly burying itself in the wall close to Shawn.

As the shocking echoes thundered along the canyon of buildings, Starbuck hurriedly set the double-barrel aside and spun to face Arlie Bishop, jarred into further consciousness by the deafening blasts. The lawman was staring at him blankly.

"What—"

Starbuck snatched the star from his shirt front, returned it to its place on Bishop's vest. "Over there—by the door—quick!" he snapped.

The lawman's eyes began to focus as his forehead pulled into an angry frown. "That was Max Eagle . . . You shot him—tricked me—"

"Get to the door!" Starbuck repeated impatiently. "And pick up that shotgun!"

The lawman moved away from the desk slowly, uncertainly. Shawn caught him by the shoulder and shoved roughly. "I don't hold with lying," he said in a tight voice, "but you lied to get this job—and for a good reason. Now you're going to lie once more! You're going to let everybody think you shot down Eagle. Won't be any need to say it—folks seeing you standing there with that shotgun in your hands will think it. You let them go on thinking it—understand?"

The sound of running in the street was growing louder. Bishop took up the double-barrel, frowning. "But somebody may've seen you—"

"Nobody did. I stood inside the doorway."

Bishop opened the weapon and replaced the spent shell. "I told you I had to do this myself," he said in a low voice.

"You'd never have made it," Starbuck replied, equally quiet. "And you're too good a man to waste. This town needs a top marshal, and you fill the bill. By the time another Max Eagle comes along you'll have enough gun savvy to meet him on even terms."

The crowd was suddenly at the door, milling about in the street and on the landing, voicing congratulations. It parted briefly and Carla burst through. Her features were slack with relief as she ran to Arlie, flung herself upon him, and began to sob brokenly. "Thank God—oh, thank God!"

Bishop held her close, soothing her as best he could. After a moment he raised his glance to Shawn and nodded slightly, his eyes expressing his thanks.

Albers, Rufe Hagerty, even Henry Grissom, with a half a dozen more of the town merchants in tow, were crowding into the office, all smiling, offering their hands. Bishop disengaged himself from Carla, pushed her gently toward the back of the room where Starbuck stood, and turned to accept the felicitations.

"Never figured you could do it," Grissom said. "And I'm big enough to admit right now in front of everybody that I was wrong—all the way."

"Far as all of us are concerned," Albers added, "that star's yours long as you want it."

Starbuck felt Carla's steady gaze upon him, quiet and searching. He looked at her and smiled. "He'll make a good lawman. You'll be proud of him."

"I am already," she replied, "thanks to you."

There was a slight hesitancy in her last words, as if she suspected there was more to the situation than met the eye. He gave her doubt short shrift.

"Had it in him all the time. Just needed somebody like Max Eagle to bring it out."

The prisoners in the adjoining room were setting up a racket, stamping the floor and banging against the bars of the cell. Shawn, relieved for an excuse to get away from Carla, stepped to the door and opened it wide. The

133

noise ceased immediately.

"What's going on out there?" Letterman demanded, craning his neck to see. "Did Max—"

"He's dead," Starbuck said flatly.

The foreman's jaw dropped. "You saying the marshal gunned him down?"

Shawn pointed to Bishop, still holding the doublebarrel in his hand as the townspeople continued to crowd in and pour out their congratulations.

"Have a look for yourself," he said, and turned back into the office.

Avoiding Carla, now in conversation with Clint Albers, he circled through the press to the door and moved out into the softening sunlight. Two men were picking up the body of the gunman, and attended by more onlookers, were starting down the street. Unnoticed, Starbuck crossed to the Far West, plucked the key to the room he'd not been able to use from the wall board, and getting his gear, made his way to the stable.

The hostler was nowhere to be found. Leaving a dollar on the table of his quarters to pay for the sorrel's care, Shawn moved down the line of stalls until he located the gelding. Saddling and bridling quickly, he backed the big horse into the runway and swung aboard . . . He could make Silver City by daylight if he pushed hard . . . Abruptly, he drew in. Arlie Bishop was standing in the doorway.

"Never got a chance to thank you proper like," the lawman said, stepping in close, hand extended.

"No need," Shawn said, clasping Arlie's fingers.

"Plenty of need. I owe everything to you—right from the start . . . You in a hurry to pull out?"

Shawn nodded. "Think my brother might be in Silver

City. Going to take a ride up there."

"I see," Bishop said thoughtfully. "When I saw you slip out of the office, I was afraid you were leaving. Had to catch you, tell you thanks—tell you, too, that I don't aim to live this lie for long. I'll tell—"

"Keeping quiet a few more months won't make any difference," Starbuck interrupted. "Hold off until you're sure of yourself, then get it off your mind. Owe that much to your wife—and the town."

Bishop smiled. "You've been right in everything else, expect you're right in this. Coming back this way?"

"Doubt it."

"Well, if you do, latch string's out at my house, always will be. Want you to know that."

"Appreciate that," Starbuck said, roweling the sorrel lightly. "Tell Carla so long for me—and take care of her."

The lawman stepped aside. "I'll do that . . . Good luck."

24

STARBUCK RODE INTO SILVER CITY just as the sun began to spread its flare behind the Mimbres Peaks in the east. Most of the hundred or so buildings that made up the town were dark, but a few of the saloons were open, and guiding the sorrel into the hitchrack of the largest, the Red Onion, he halted and swung down.

Dust covered his clothing and had laid a gray film on his features; otherwise, there was no visible evidence of the hard ride he'd made as he stepped up onto the saloon's landing and paused to glance around.

A half block down, a small pavilion had been erected, its fresh-cut timbers covered with red and white bunting. At one corner of the raised platform a bell had been suspended from a hangman's post. Tiered bleachers faced the arrangement on all four sides.

Letterman had been right; he was looking at the ring where a boxing match had taken place. Pulse quickening, he moved on hurriedly, opened the door of the Red Onion, which had been closed to ward off the chill of night, and entered.

Evidently it had been a big night in the silver-rich settlement. More than two dozen men were sleeping in the broad, square room—some slumped in chairs, some draped across tables, others simply stretched out on the sawdust-covered floor. The bartender was no exception. Starbuck, crossing to the long counter, located the man dozing in a round-backed chair tipped against the wall behind it.

Circling to the man's side, Shawn shook him awake. "I can use a drink—rye," he said.

The saloonkeeper rocked forward and came slowly to his feet. He stared numbly at Starbuck while the words seeped into his fogged brain and finally registered.

"Rye," he mumbled, and moved up to the counter.

Shawn, again on the customer's side of the bar, downed the liquor in a single gulp, remaining silent for a moment as the whiskey built a warmth within him.

"Fight's all over, I see," he said, finally.

The bartender yawned, then nodded. "Yesterday noon."

"Who won?"

"That boxer fellow. Cut Jess Wilkins into cat meat. Never seen such a mess—and Jess outweighing him a hundred pounds!"

"The boxer," Starbuck said, pushing back his glass for a refill, "what was his name?"

The bartender unsteadily tipped the bottle he held, dribbling a quantity of its contents into the thick-bottomed glass. "Friend," he said, shaking his head. "Sure was a lot of money changed hands over that fight. Nobody figured he'd whip Jess."

It was Ben—it had to be . . . Drink untouched, Shawn leaned forward, trail-stained features intent, voice carefully controlled to mask the rising hope within him. "You know if he's still around?"

"Jess? Yeh, he's—"

"Not him—Friend."

The bartender yawned again, wagging his head. "Naw, he lit out right afterwards. Grabbed his money and was long gone."

Starbuck lowered his eyes and stared moodily into the amber liquid filling his glass. He had missed out again.

"Heard it said why he was in such a powerful hurry," the bartender continued in a confidential tone. "Seems there was some gamblers wanting him to throw the fight so's they could clean up big. He flat wouldn't do it. Told them so, but they threatened him, trying to make him do it anyways.

"Didn't scare him none. He just went right ahead, done a job on Jess, collected his cash, and took off . . . All this was told to me, you understand. I ain't saying it's the truth, only that I heard—"

"I savvy," Shawn said wearily, reassuring the man. "Anybody asks me, I'll say I don't remember who told me."

Raising his glass, he swallowed the rye, trying to shake off the heaviness that gripped him. He'd failed before and likely he'd do so again before the search finally ended. Disappointment was an old, familiar companion.

"You know which way he was heading when he rode out?"

"West, somebody said." The bartender paused. "You're a mite anxious about him. Mind telling me why? He owe you or something?"

"No. I'm pretty sure he's my brother."

"Do tell!" the saloonman exclaimed in a surprised voice. He leaned forward, squinting at Starbuck through the weak lamp light. "By hell, you do look sort've like him! He ain't tall as you, and he's a bit heavier and built thicker through the shoulders—but the face is sure pretty much the same."

Shawn settled back slowly on his heels, a feeling of satisfaction running through him. He had arrived too late, but he had accomplished one thing; the last shred of doubt that Damon Friend was Ben had been erased.

"Big shame you didn't get here sooner," the bartender said. "He sure did put on a show."

Starbuck nodded, reaching into his pocket for a coin. He was suddenly dog-tired, hungry—and wanting to hear no more.

"How much?"

"Be a dollar."

He raised no objection to the outrageous price, dug for another coin, and laying it on the counter, turned for the door. Ben had pointed west, the saloonman had said . . . West that meant Arizona. Sighing, he moved through the doorway and stepped out into the cold, crisp morning. He'd stable the sorrel, get a bite to eat, and rest for a while. Then he'd move on. Maybe his luck would be better the next time.

We hope that you enjoyed reading this
Sagebrush Large Print Western.
If you would like to read more Sagebrush titles,
ask your librarian or contact the Publishers:

United States and Canada

Thomas T. Beeler, *Publisher*
Post Office Box 310
Rollinsford, New Hampshire 03869-0310
(800) 818-7574

United Kingdom, Eire, and
the Republic of South Africa

Isis Publishing Ltd
7 Centremead
Osney Mead
Oxford OX2 0ES England
(01865) 250333

Australia and New Zealand

Bolinda Publishing Pty. Ltd.
17 Mohr Street
Tullamarine, 3043, Victoria, Australia
(016103) 9338 0666